The Neriu
The All-

A A Lockwood

This is a work of fiction. Names, characters, places, and incidents either are the product of the author's imagination or are used fictitiously. Any resemblance to actual persons, living or dead, events, or locales is entirely coincidental.

First paperback edition October 2023

Book design by A A Lockwood

ISBN 979-8-8644-5841-9 (paperback)

ISBN 979-8-8646-2756-3 (hardcover)

The Nerium Tales: The All-Power

A A Lockwood

For Kristy, one of my closest friends who finished this story first.

And for Tracy, my sister whom I love dearly, who read it next.

1

It was one of those dimly lit bars that chose not to play music, the type that was popular with drinkers in their early twenties, the type of bar they would all go to before going to a club where they would all pretend that they had not already been discretely eyeballing each other all night. It was busy, so busy that it really did not matter whether music was playing or not, there were so many conversations going on that they all rose and combined to create a dull roar that filled the bar. Aaron hated it.

At one end of the bar was a group of women in their early to mid-twenties, drinking and talking and laughing, paying no attention to anyone else in the place. Or that would be how it looked to anyone that was not paying attention. They were drinking and talking and laughing, that was true, but they were definitely paying attention to the other drinkers. They were paying careful attention to the group of men at the other end of the bar, the group of men who were doing the exact same thing. Aaron watched from within his own group, trying hard to remember the last time he had done that. It must have been almost twenty years ago.

Elsewhere in the bar there were other noticeable groups. Groups of couples, they were always the ones desperate to sit down. Groups of singles wandering around, mingling and chatting with other groups of singles. A group of men stood quietly in the corner, those were the ones who had started drinking later than most of the other drinkers, they were the ones that wanted a good night out but weren't quite drunk enough to talk to people they didn't know, not just yet anyway.

And stood around a table close to the bar was a group that, if someone were to look carefully, they would be able to tell that it was a group of work friends. This group was all men and their ages ranged from late teens to late forties. They weren't just work friends though, these work friends were all in the Army. These work friends were more like brothers, even the youngest and newest member that was fresh out of training, he had yet to prove himself, and they reminded him of that fact at every given opportunity, but he was one of them. Tonight, this group was out to celebrate one of their longest serving members. Aaron Scott.

Aaron Scott had been in the Army since he was eighteen, tomorrow was his forty second birthday, and his last working day in the military. Twenty four years in the service, he had never known any other life and he was, quite understandably, nervous about leaving the life behind. He had heard a lot of stories about people struggling to switch from soldier to civilian, he had been in situations that a lot of people would call scary but what scared him right now was the thought of having to go through job interviews again. He worried that if employers noticed that his CV pointed out that he had been in the Army for twenty four years they would immediately think that he was aggressive and violent, or maybe they would assume that he would not respect their authority. He was not aggressive or violent, far from it, in fact he could hardly remember the last time he had got angry at something, or even raised his voice. Also, he understood that if he went somewhere where he did not know everything, he could learn from the people that did know everything in that speciality, and to him it did not matter if they were young or old – if they knew more than him, he could learn from them.

He had fought hard throughout his career to help others see that way, when he had first joined the Army a lot of people would immediately dismiss the ideas of newer soldiers with comments like. "What do you know, you've only been in five minutes."

It had taken years of hard work and proving himself before he could make others see that it did not matter how long someone had been in the Army for their ideas to matter and that thinking differently was not always a bad thing. But he did not know how to get all of that across to a potential employer in a short interview, if he even got an interview to begin with.

But, for tonight he had pushed those worries aside, tonight he was only worrying about the hangover he was going to have for the next three days. When the youngest member of his group appeared with a tray full of brightly coloured shots, he saw that as a sign that it was time for him to disappear, he told them he was going to the bathroom and gave a quick nod to one of his older friends who knew exactly what Aaron was about to do, and he left.

The roar of conversation was replaced by a high pitched ringing noise in the back of his ears the moment he stepped out of the building, the tone that came from a mix of alcohol and the sudden silence whenever you left a noisy pub. He staggered to the nearest taxi rank, hopped into the first one he saw and gave the driver his address before happily letting out a sigh of relief.

"Heavy night?" The driver chuckled.

Aaron looked at him and tried his hardest to keep him in focus. "Heavy enough to feel it for the next few days, my birthday tomorrow so the guys wanted to celebrate." Aaron let out a burp. "Forty two, how did that happen?"

"Well, you must have had an easy paper round, you don't look that old. What's your secret?" Laughed the driver.

It was not the first time Aaron had been asked. "No Mrs, and a nice quiet house to go home to." He replied and the two laughed and chatted some more until Aaron paid the driver and got out to stumble to his house, he did not make it that far. As he was walking away from the taxi, the clock struck midnight and Aaron dropped to the ground. Dead.

Or that was how it looked to the taxi driver and to the curtain twitchers peeking out to see who was driving up the quiet street at midnight.

And also, how it looked to Aaron, who was suddenly stood staring down at his own body lying on the ground. He knew he should be afraid, but at that moment he was not, in that moment all he felt was calm. Then he saw the taxi driver get out of the car and run over to his body. He saw a light come on in his neighbours' house, he saw another neighbour come rushing out of her house with her phone in her hand. Then he saw the scene in front of him get smaller as he was pulled upwards and backwards through the air. He saw his whole street, his whole town, his whole country, the world, the moon. He was pulled backwards faster and faster, until all he could see was small specks of light streaking past him in straight lines, reminding him of the science fiction movies he liked to watch but would never have admitted to his friends. Then everything went dark as he lost consciousness.

2

The next thing Aaron knew, he was waking up in a large hall with smooth looking black walls lit by flaming torches. He was surrounded by kids wearing long black robes, all sat in neat lines, and they all looked to be waking up as well, their confused looks mirroring the confusion he was feeling. After a few moments he noticed movement on a small stage at the front of the hall, four women and two men, who all looked to be in their fifties, were walking in from a door he had not noticed. These new people were also wearing long robes, their robes however, were not black. One of the women wearing sky blue robes stepped to the front of the small stage and cleared her throat to get the attention of the seated kids and Aaron, needlessly, as every eye in the hall was already on her.

"Good morning everyone, I am Head Mistress Taylor. I am sure you all have a lot of questions but please save them for now as I will endeavour to give you answers before you need to ask them. You are currently at Doctrina School on Nerium." She paused as confused kids turned to look at each other obviously trying to see if this statement made any sense to anyone. Once everyone was looking at her again, she continued. "One hundred children are selected at birth every year from all over the world and, for centuries, once those children reached the age of sixteen, they were taken from Earth and brought here." More confused looks and quite a few murmurs at that point. "Save your questions." The head mistress said with so much authority that she immediately silenced the hall. "That is, until one hundred and thirty years ago when a woman named Margaret Proctor became the Prime Mage. Margaret Proctor remembered being ripped from Earth at such a young age and the pain of never being able to see her family again, as the only way to cross from Earth to Nerium is to become a student, there is, as far as anyone knows, no way to return to Earth from Nerium. She used the memory of that pain throughout her election campaign, it turned out that many of the voters also remembered and agreed with her. Her first act as the Prime was to change things, allowing new students to live a full life on Earth and with their families, those children would live to the age of forty two, before being taken from Earth and starting school here on Nerium, there was one little drawback though." She took a breath and smiled understandingly out into the hall. "I am sure you have all noticed that you are once again in your 16-year-old body."

Aaron had not in fact noticed this, but he did now, he looked at his hands noticing how much younger they looked, he rolled the sleeves of his robes back to see no tattoos, he reached up to find his chin stubble free, and now that he thought about it, there was a distinct lack of knee pain. At this point the five other people on the stage that had not yet introduced themselves started walking through the neat rows and placed drinks on each of the desks of the shocked adults in teenage bodies, when one of them reached Aaron, he noticed that the drink seemed to appear out of nowhere. Aaron accepted the drink with a nod of thanks, he was not sure what the drink was, but it tasted vaguely like very sweet coffee, Aaron did not mind and happily drank it. As he felt the hot, bitter and sweet liquid rush down his throat, the sudden shock of finding himself in his teenage body seemed to lessen. He looked around the hall, realising for the first time that all of the kids surrounding him were all like him, they weren't kids at all. They were all forty two years old and suddenly a teenager again. He continued drinking and by the time he had finished the drink he was eager to hear more from this Head Mistress Taylor. He looked around to see all the drinks were finished and all the seated faces looked calmer.

The Head Mistress continued. "Nerium is a world very similar to Earth, only without technology. And it has magic, as do all of you."

A lot of murmurs broke out at this point, and a voice spoke from the crowd behind Aaron. "Magic? That's ridiculous!"

The Head Mistress did not miss a beat. "No more ridiculous than suddenly being in your teenage bodies again. Save your questions." She said in the direction of the voice, no reply came, and the murmurs silenced, she carried on. "Doctrina School is where you will live for the next three to four years while you learn to use and control your own branch of magic. Your lessons will begin on Monday, today, by the way, is Friday. This is done to give you all a few days to get used to being in this magical world, your refreshed bodies and to do any pre reading you would like to do." Several hands raised at this point. "Save your questions. Once you have all discovered your branch, your room will appear in the accommodation wing, in your room will be everything you will need for this year, including books for pre reading." She paused here and Aaron noticed some of the people that had raised their hands relax their shoulders. “You will all discover your branch of magic within the next hour. Once that is done you will be taught by a professor who shares that branch.” She gestured to four of the others standing on the stage. “Professor Hawthorn will teach the Earth mages.” She introduced a short balding man wearing dark green robes who then walked off the stage and to the back right corner of the hall. “Professor Fray the Air mages.” A tall skinny woman, wearing the same sky blue robes as the head mistress, she followed the first professor off the stage and went to the front right corner of the hall. “Professor Quail teaches the Water mages.” A rather strict looking man wearing deep blue robes that went to the front left corner. “And Professor Gibson the Fire mages.” A woman with blood red robes and long ginger hair with an orange glint in her eyes, she almost glided to the back left corner of the massive room. “Now, I am about to go through each of the specialities within each branch. As I explain each one, you will begin to feel a tingle, something like pins and needles, once that feeling covers your entire body, you will have discovered your branch and your speciality within that branch. If you do not notice that feeling, Professor Fray and I, are able to see your auras and we will inform you. Once you have discovered your branch, you will move to stand in a corner of the hall where your new branch professor is waiting. If any of that is unclear to anyone, it will make sense soon.”

She began to break down the Earth branch and as soon as she started to explain the first speciality Aaron noticed his fingertips beginning to tingle. Once she had finished explaining the Plant speciality the first person stood up and walked over to where Professor Hawthorn was standing. As the Head Mistress worked through all the other Earth specialities Aarons tingle slowly expanded to cover up to his elbows, as it was definitely not covering his entire body, Aaron stayed sitting where he was. As Head Mistress Taylor began to go through the Air branch, Aarons toes began to tingle. When the Air branch had been fully explained, Aaron's tingle had grown up to his knees. At that point, his hands to his elbow and his feet to his knees were tingling, not his full body, again he remained sitting where he was. Aaron was beginning to feel a little confused. By the time the Water branch had been fully explained, Aarons whole arms were tingling along with his lower legs, he began to look around to see if anyone else looked as confused as he felt. Once the Head Mistress was finished with the Fire branch Aarons arms and legs were covered with the tingle.

By this time only ten people remained seated, the Head Mistress did not seem worried. "And then there are the Healers. Continue listening and if you discover you are a healer, please stand with Professor Iaso." She introduced the final professor on the stage, who wore white robes, she looked to be in her thirties but had a full head of grey hair, she smiled at those that remained seated and moved to stand in front of the stage. The head mistress continued on to explain the healer branch, when she was finished four people stood and moved to stand with Professor Iaso, the head mistress smiled and continued. "And then there are those special mages who have a dual speciality, as I go through these, when you know you have discovered your duality, come and stand in front of the stage." She began with the Earth Water combination, a forty two year old teenaged girl and a teenaged adult boy stood and walked to stand in front of the stage. The Head Mistress smiled at the two of them and continued with Air Fire, at this point the other three stood, they also moved to stand in front of the stage. Leaving Aaron sat alone, his tingle now covering his arms, legs and up to his navel. The Head Mistress moved onto the rare Earth Air, and the even rarer Water Fire. Aarons tingle now covered up to his shoulders, leaving only his head 'untingled'. He looked to the Head Mistress and was a little surprised to see the look of shock, and maybe a little fear on her face, he looked around the hall and saw the same look on all five of the professors. The Head Mistress had composed herself by the time Aaron looked back to her. "And then there is the rarest of all, one that has not been seen on Nerium for almost one hundred and fifty years. The All-Power."

Immediately Aarons tingle grew to cover his entire body, the force of the full body tingle pulled him to a standing position. He stayed standing where he was, alone in the centre of the hall. After a few moments of silence where one hundred adult teenagers looked towards the professors waiting for some form of direction, the head mistress continued, her eyes still on Aaron.

"Excellent, now that you all know which Branch and speciality you are. You can now head off to the accommodation wing to find your new rooms. Please follow Professor Gibson." She pointed to the back of the hall where Professor Gibson was now stood by a door.

Aaron joined the masses but looked back before leaving the hall to see Head Mistress Taylor and the remaining Professors all with the shocked, fearful look back on their faces. They were all looking directly at him.

3

Aaron walked along with the group of confused new students, taking note of each turn, right out of the hall, left into an open courtyard, to the end of the courtyard and left again, walk about fifty metres and then into the accommodation wing. Easy enough.

Professor Gibson did not enter with them, instead she simply stood by the door as they all walked in past her, Aaron did not look at her to see if she had the same expression on her face as the professors he had left behind in the hall.

When he got into the accommodation wing, he saw he was in a very big common room area that was already filled with about two hundred people, most of whom were wearing the same varied coloured robes as the Professor's Aaron had just met, clearly the second and third year students, they had set the room up ready for a party, complete with food and drink and a large banner that read. 'Welcome new students.' But they were all stood silently staring at the new arrivals, and they had the same shocked look on their faces as the professors had.

A girl with deep blue robes, Aaron assumed this meant she was a Water mage, towards the front of the welcoming group nervously stepped forward.

"The All-Power door opened up." She said, and she pointed towards a wall to the left of the entrance where eight doors stood next to each other, so close to each other that Aaron did not think that there could be anything more than a cupboard behind each door. “Who’s the All-Power?”

Aaron took a few steps forward. “I am. What’s the big deal? All the Professors looked worried, so do most of you. What’s the problem?” He had not meant for it to sound quite as confrontational as it came out, but he thought that if he did not ask why being an ‘All-Power’ was worrying to everyone straight away, he might not find out.

“No, no not worried, it’s just super rare. That’s all.” The girl turned towards the welcoming group, Aaron got the impression that she was wordlessly telling them all to act normally. When she turned back, she had a smile on her face. “Go find your rooms and when you all come back out, we’ll get the welcome party going. Go on, we’ll be here when you get back.”

Aaron quickly scanned the group and saw quite a few people still staring at him, he decided not to let the question go. He took a few steps towards the girl that had spoken to him, before noticing her smile vanish to be replaced with, what could only be described as a look of terror, she glanced around as though she was looking for somewhere to hide. “Please?” He said to her with his hands outstretched and what he hoped was a friendly look on his face. “If we talk somewhere a little quieter, will you give me an actual answer? Please, I don’t know why everyone seems worried and why, right now, you look scared of me. I just want to know.” He asked pleadingly.

She looked at Aaron for a moment then gave him a tight smile. "OK, find your room and I'll be here when you come back out. It shouldn't be difficult, yours will be the only one in there."

Aaron thanked her and turned back to where the doors were to see his fellow new students piling into them. The crowd had thinned by the time he got close to them, so he got a clear look at each door. The three doors on the left were plain, ordinary looking doors. The first had the word Earth written on it, the second had Water and on the third was written Earth Water. Aaron presumed that was for the Earth Water dual mages, next there was a space in the wall big enough for another two doors and then a large, extremely ornate door with the words All-Power carved into it. Next to the All-Power door, Aaron's door, the doors returned to the plain, ordinary looking doors. The first had Air Fire written on it, another dual mage door. Then another space big enough for another door, a door with Air written on it, then a Water door. And finally, a door with Healer written on it. Aaron walked to his door and pushed it open, he was surprised to see a corridor with another door at the end and not a cupboard. He walked on and into his new room and was surprised again. He was unsure what he had been expecting, but what he saw was not it. He was looking at a room filled with books with a sofa and an armchair in the middle and a desk and chair in a corner, there was another door to his right, in through there was a big bed that looked very comfortable with drawers and wardrobes filled with an assortment of robes, his robes were not the singular blocks of colours he had seen, and they were also all of the colours at the same time. His robes reminded him of the combats he wore in the Army, except that they were, to his eyes, almost offensively colourful with large swathes of colours. He took a disgusted look at them and decided then to keep wearing the black ones. There was another door in his bedroom that led into a very well-furnished bathroom, this was not a 'room', this was almost a whole flat, all that was missing was a kitchen.

Aaron walked back through into what he decided to call his library and scanned the shelves. There were books on all the branches and specialities, then one particular book caught his eye.

An accurate history of The All-Power – for All-Power eyes only.

He ran a finger down it's spine before deciding not to look at it then, but to go and get the answer he had been promised instead.

He could hear the group in the common room as he walked back down his little corridor, as soon as he opened his door, they once again went silent. He quickly looked around and noticed that he was the first to come back out of the doors, not surprising really, they had all gone in as branch groups. Aaron assumed they were talking about their rooms and generally chatting. He looked back to the silent staring group and knew he had to put a stop to this. "Alright stop! It might be rare, but this is ridiculous." Once again, he did not mean for it to sound quite so confrontational. But it seemed to work, most of them turned away and they slowly started talking to each other. Aaron knew they were talking about him but at least they weren't staring silently anymore.

There were still a few people staring however, one in particular caught Aaron's eye, a short dark-haired boy wearing the same blood red robes as Professor Gibson, a boy who looked to be about eighteen, a third year. This boy was unashamedly staring at him, but the thing that grabbed Aaron's attention was the fact that this boy was the only one that did not have a worried look on his face, this boy looked excited. That was more concerning to Aaron than two hundred people looking worried and scared, what was going on in that boys' head, what was he planning.

Aaron was still considering this when the first of the other first year students started coming out of their corridors and the boy finally looked away. As the two groups began to mingle and started chatting, the new students finding out whatever they could about this strange new world and this strange school. Aaron looked around to find the girl, she was sat in a corner of the common room waiting for him to seek her out, she gestured to the empty armchair next to her. Aaron walked over and sat down.

"How long do you think it will be before people stop staring at me?" He asked as he sunk into the armchair.

"Keep shouting at them like that and they might keep staring." She replied nervously.

"What? I didn't shout." He said, genuinely surprised. "Think about it from my perspective. Last night I was out on the piss with my friends celebrating my forty second birthday. This morning I wake up in a weird hall, in weird clothes, find out I'm sixteen, that I'm not on Earth, that I'm going to magic school and I have some special power that no one has seen in a hundred and fifty years. And to top all of that off, everyone is worried, scared or in the case of one of the faces I've just seen – excited. I don't understand what's happening. I've been here for a few hours and people have done nothing but stare. If I say nothing, they'll just keep staring." Aaron sighed and shook his head. "I just want to know why. I'm Aaron by the way." He added an introduction, a little later in the conversation than he normally would have done.

She smiled at him, an actual smile this time. "I'm Heidi. A third year, and prefect. It's my job to welcome you all today." She looked around the common room and nodded to herself. "Ok." She muttered as though she was mentally preparing herself to say whatever she was about to say. "Ok, one of the first lessons we all have when we start here is a history of Nerium. You learn about various wars that have been fought here. And, well, they were all started by an All-Power. The last war ended one hundred and fifty years ago, it took seventy mages from all branches to defeat the last All-Power. Think about that, a battle between seventy mages and one All-Power. And it nearly wasn't enough. That's why everyone seems worried." Heidi looked worried again, but this time she was not worried about Aaron, but worried for him.

Aaron laughed and looked at her in disbelief. "I have literally just got here. You are the only person I have spoken to. And you're telling me that everyone thinks I'm going to start a war." He laughed. "That's the craziest thing I've heard all day. And that really is saying something." Aaron looked around the room and caught a few people quickly looking away. "Here's an idea, if for some reason I go loopy and try starting a war. How about no one joins my Army. That way I'm just a nutter." He tried to make a joke of it.

"That's the thing Aaron. None of them had an army, every All-Power that's ever started a war has been their own Army. The history books say that there isn't much an All-Power can't do." She said sadly.

Aaron shook his head in disbelief. "There must've been All-Powers that haven't started a war, you know, just had a normal life, and stayed out of the history books. Trust me, I'm not the war starting type."

"Maybe, but the only ones in the history books are bad guys. I'm sorry, but that's why everyone's staring and looking worried. I hope you're right and you won't start a war, but I've given you the answer you asked for, I have to get back to the party and meet the new Water mages. Sorry." She smiled again and disappeared into the crowd.

Aaron sat back in his chair and tried to take in what Heidi had just told him while he watched the new students mingle with the crowd of older students, asking questions and getting to know people. Then he saw the boy again, staring straight at him. He started walking towards Aaron, Aaron did not move from his chair. Whatever this boy wanted to get off his chest could not be any worse than what Heidi had just told Aaron.

"I'm going to be a hero." The boy shouted as he got closer to Aaron.

"Excuse me?" Aaron replied, not in any mood for something like this.

"Nerium will throw me parades when they find out I killed an All-Power before he had chance to start anything."

"Wait! What?" Aaron did not have chance to say anything else as the boy pointed the palms of his hands at him and shot a stream of flames. Straight out of his hands. Straight at Aarons head. Aaron instinctively raised his hands in defence, palms facing the boy, and was amazed to see the flames being absorbed into his own palms. He felt them race through his muscles and through his veins, the flames coursing within him, giving him a feeling of power he had never known. The room was silent as Aaron stared at his hands and the boy looked shocked. Aaron looked up at the boy and was filled with sudden anger, as though the flames he had just absorbed had taken all of their heat and turned it into a rage he had never felt. He stood up with such force that the armchair fell over behind him, the boy took several terrified steps backwards and fell over his own feet. "What the hell is wrong with you?" He roared at the boy. "I have been here for a few hours, I know one person's name in this entire room. And you try to kill me!" Inside his mind, Aaron could see himself launch the flames back at the boy, scorching him to a crisp, he could even imagine the smell of the boys charred flesh stinging his nose. He shook his head to lose the thought, took a breath to calm himself and turned to the crowd, not one of them seemed concerned by what the boy had just done. But they were all staring at Aaron again. "None of you know me, not one of you." He shouted into the crowd, this time he knew that he was shouting at them, but he did not care. "But you all assume I'm going to end up being some sort of crazy super villain. Why not try getting to know me before trying to kill me?" Not one of them moved. "You know what, fine! Stare all you want!" Aaron walked towards the table that had been set up full of food and drinks, the crowd parting as he got close to them. He grabbed as much as he could carry and stormed backed to his room.

4

Aaron dumped everything onto his desk and dropped onto the sofa shaking his head, hardly able to believe anything that had happened today. Yesterday he was worrying about leaving the Army and being able to find a new job, now, not fifty feet away there were two hundred people afraid he was going to start a war. No doubt the ninety nine other first year students would start to think that soon as well. Heidi might not be right, he thought, surely not every All-Power in history could have started a war.

"They couldn't have all been bad. I'm not, I know I'm not." He said aloud to his empty library and his bookshelves, then he spotted the book that had caught his eye.

An accurate history of The All-Power – for All-Power eyes only

Aaron got up and picked the book from the shelf. He sat back down and gingerly opened it to its first page.

When humans first appeared on Nerium there was an All-Power.

The first All-Power.

Isabella Lockton, all the lesser mages grew to fear her, simply because she was more than them.

She made a prophecy, the only prophecy ever made in Neriums recorded history.

"There will be an All-Power that will rule Nerium for eternity, they will teach this world the meaning of fear."

It has never been clear whether this is a true prophecy or the angry words of a persecuted All-Power.

Table of contents

1. *Isabella Lockton*
2. *Nicholas Garnier*
3. *Aban Fasil*
4. *Anastasia Solovyov*
5. *Henry Carmine*
6. *Alexander Miller*
7. *Aaron Scott*

Aaron stopped and stared at the last name on the page. His name. In a book. That could not be his name, there must have been another All-Power with the same name. He threw the pages over to reach the last chapter.

Aaron Scott 763 –

That was it. The entire chapter. Maybe it was his name, but how could it be in this book? He decided that was a question for another time. He flipped backwards through the pages to the beginning of the chapter before.

Alexander Miller 527 – 613

Alexander Millers story began like most other All-Powers with the exception of the First.

From the moment of his All-Power discovery, he felt the fear from the lesser mages, throughout his years at Doctrina he suffered attack after attack. From his professors as well as his fellow students, he emerged from every attack unscathed and not once did he return the aggression. Instead opting to defend only.

Once his studies at Doctrina were completed, in the year 531 Alexander Miller chose to live in isolation.

In isolation he remained until the year 587 when a group of newly graduated students found him, they had heard tales of an All-Power living in the woods near the town of Senin, and they took it upon themselves to save Nerium from the All-Power menace. It did not matter to them that Alexander Miller had been living peacefully and alone for fifty six years. Doctrina had taught them that All-Powers were a danger to Nerium. The group, seven in total approached Alexander Miller at his home, and after several declarations of his want for peaceful solitude, the group attacked Alexander Miller. Once again Alexander Miller opted to defend only, but the group kept attacking and attacking and attacking. Until Alexander Miller lost his temper for the first time on Nerium. With a wave of his arm, all seven attackers fell dead.

Alexander Miller was filled with remorse for what he had done, for the lives he had taken. Alexander Miller carried the seven bodies to Senin and laid them carefully on the ground. The people of the town would not listen to Alexander Millers explanation of the events. They instead chose to believe that Alexander Miller had spent his years in isolation formulating a plan to lay waste to Nerium and that he had finally decided to act on his plan.

The people of Senin went to the Prime Mage of the time and gave him their version of events, claiming that Alexander Miller had stood over the bodies of those that he had slain declaring. "More is to come."

The Prime Mage sent ten lesser mages to kill Alexander Miller. The lesser mage kill squad chose to wait until night when Alexander Miller was asleep and defenceless, and they attacked. This time, out of fear Alexander Miller waved his arm and the kill squad fell dead.

Knowing that his peaceful isolation was over, Alexander Miller fled, attempting to find a new place of isolation. The Prime Mage however, declared war against Alexander Miller, and he pursued the peaceful All-Power all over Nerium for twenty six years where the same thing happened time after time. The attackers chose to attack the sleeping defenceless Alexander Miller. Every time Alexander Miller woke in fear and reactively, never intentionally, killed all the attackers before leaving to once again find isolation.

This continued until the Prime Mage decided to join his largest kill squad yet. A total of seventy lesser mages approached Alexander Millers latest attempt at isolation and confronted him, this time choosing not to wait until he slept. Alexander Miller begged and pleaded with the lesser mages stating that he acted in self defence and out of fear.

But the Prime Mage did not listen and attacked, sending wave after wave of attackers at Alexander Miller from all sides. The Prime Mage lost fifty seven of the lesser mages until one chose not to use magic and stabbed Alexander Miller repeatedly in the back. Alexander Miller tried to relay to the Prime Mage that persecution and hatred was not the way, but he died before he could say more than. "One day you will learn".

Alexander Miller was murdered in the year 613 at the young age of 102.

Aaron sat back to digest what he had just read, the repeated use of the term 'lesser mages' told him that this was nothing more than propaganda. Yet, if this was propaganda, it seemed oddly catered to him. Aaron had spent his entire military career trying to rid his battalion of hatred and persecution, to encourage and embrace diversity. But there were the attacks against Alexander at Doctrina, Aaron had only been at Doctrina for a few hours and had already had to defend himself against an attack. Aaron did not know what to think. He needed some air, he grabbed some things that looked like sausage rolls from his desk and left his room. Once again, the common room went silent as soon as he entered but this time, Aaron did not bother to acknowledge it, instead he turned to the exit and walked out.

Aaron knew that if he turned to the right, he would end up back at the courtyard that led to the hall he had arrived here in. To his left, he saw more buildings but in front of him was an open field with a single tree devoid of any leaves.

Aaron let out a little chuckle, remembering punishments in the Army – if his section had messed up or even said the wrong thing to the section commander, they would hear the words. “Lone tree. Go!” And the whole section would have to sprint to the tree and back, sometimes having to apologise to the tree. With the chuckle still on his lips, Aaron set off walking towards the tree.

He had not gone twenty steps before he heard someone call out behind him. “Hey, wait!” Aaron turned to see three people, a tall skinny Indian boy and two girls, coming out of the accommodation wing. He recognised them as the three Air Fire dual mages, the last three to stand in the hall they had arrived in before he had. The story of Alexander Miller still running through his mind, Aaron was immediately on edge expecting an attack, but he waited. “Hi, I’m Amelie.” The taller girl introduced herself. “This is Tala.” She pointed to a short smiling Asian girl. “And that’s Ajit.” She introduced the boy last. Aaron made no move to respond. Amelie continued. “We’re first years too.” She said with a smile, Aaron still did not respond. “Yeah, those guys in there have told us ‘You’ll learn this, and you’ll learn that’, but we agree with you. We should probably get to know someone before judging them. You’re Aaron, right?”

Aaron sighed and shook his head. “Heidi’s already been telling everyone about me, has she?”

“Yes, but not in a bad way.” Tala replied to him this time. “When you went back into your room she started screaming at Dylan, that’s the boy who attacked you, and she told him that he was going to be reported for attempted murder. Then she turned to everyone else and told us that we should listen to you, that’s when she said your name, and we should try to be friends with you because you seemed nice. Then she grabbed Dylan and dragged him out of the common room.” She blurted out, hardly seeming to take a breath while she was talking.

“Most of the first years that we’ve spoken to agree.” Ajit continued. “If I’m being honest, I think the second and third years have been in these teenage bodies so long they’ve forgotten that they’re actually adults.”

Aaron smiled, the first smile of the day. He turned towards the tree. “I’m going to sit by that tree for a bit, you lot want to come?” The three of them smiled and started walking with him to the tree.

“Aaron, that’s a funny name. Where are you from?” Tala asked.

Aaron laughed. “No, it’s not, it’s quite a common name in England. Why? Where are you from?”

“Oh, you’re English. Shame, I like British accents.” She blurted out.

Aaron was confused. “What do you mean Shame? I definitely have a British accent.”

Tala shook her head. “Not to me, to me you’re speaking Tagalog. To Ajit you’re speaking Hindi and to Amelie you’re speaking French. According to the others in there, we’re all actually speaking Nerian, but we hear our own language. Doesn’t make any sense to me.” She shrugged.

Aaron looked at the other two to see them nodding in agreement and considered this for a minute. “That makes as much sense as anything else here.”

5

Aaron could not be sure whether he should trust his fellow first years or not, but the last thing he wanted right now on this strange new world, was to be alone.

The next morning Aaron was surprised to find that his plain black robes had vanished, leaving him with no choice but to wear the oddly coloured robes. With some embarrassment he left his room to meet his three friends, when they emerged from their corridor, they were all wearing new robes as well, theirs were not as busy as his were, theirs were just two blocks of colour, the lower half was blood red, and the top half was sky blue. The four of them walked together to the main hall for breakfast, Aaron noticed that once again, a lot of people stared at him as they walked. Once they reached the main hall, they found that there was a long queue leading to a large pot in the centre of the hall.

Heidi was stood next to the big pot, and she smiled at Aaron when he got there. "Hi, I didn't see you after what happened last night. Are you ok?"

Aaron had the sudden impression that she used to be one of those people that greeted you in a bank on Earth. "I am. I'm not sure how, but I'm fine." He smiled back at her.

“Thank goodness. I went and reported him straight away, the professors have put him in detention for a few weeks.” She smiled again, then she nodded to the pot. “Ok then, this is how most meals work here. Apart from the end of season celebrations. For those, the second years bring in food from around Nerium that the professors have collected, and there is always a feast in the common room at the start of each break, and for the arrival of the new first years. Like we had last night. But most meals work like this.” She said, now speaking to all four of the first years, a few older students waited patiently behind them. “Think about what you want to eat, grab a plate or a bowl, whatever that goes onto.”

Aaron immediately thought of a full English fry up and picked up a plate.

“Everyone calls this stuff gruel.” Heidi continued.

Aaron investigated the pot to see, what looked like very thick brown porridge, bubbling angrily. He pulled a face, suddenly not hungry.

“Don’t think about how it looks too much.” Heidi said laughing a little at the face Aaron was making. “The moment it hits your plate or bowl. It turns into whatever you’re thinking of.” She looked up at the four of them, they all stared back at her entirely unconvinced. “And do the same when you come for lunch and dinner as well.” She finished with a smile.

Aaron found that extremely difficult to believe but he grabbed hold of the ladle and lifted a scoop out. The thick substance inside attempted to keep hold of the ladle until a loud squelching, sucking sound came from the pot as he managed to lift the heavy ladle free. He looked to the other three to see them all looking a little queasy.

He tipped the brown gruel onto his plate. Just as Heidi had said, the moment it hit his plate, it changed from the unappetising brown substance to sausages, bacon, beans, hash browns, fried and scrambled eggs and toast. Aaron felt the smell of it all hit his nose and any disgust he felt from looking at the gruel was gone. “Oh wow. I could get used to this.” He said smiling and looking up to Heidi and the other three.

Sat at a table, the four of them discussed what they were having for breakfast. Tala was eating something called Hotsilog which she said was garlic fried rice, fried eggs and hotdogs. Ajit had Paratha, a flat bread with vegetable curry and yogurt sauce. And Amelie had a croissant with butter and jam. Aaron thought it was a strange sight as he could only see the brown gruel on their plates, Tala and he were using cutlery to eat but Amelie and Ajit were using their hands. Ajit was picking up bits of gruel and dipping it into other bits of gruel. A strange sight indeed.

He was still contemplating this when someone he had not met yet bent over the table, this new person had robes of dark green on his left side and deep blue on his right. “When you have finished your breakfasts, come back to the common room and sit with the rest of the dual mages.” He said to the group as a whole. Then he stood up and left the hall.

“Anyone know who that was?” Aaron asked, a little wary of this new person.

Ajit nodded, his head bowed over his plate. “I spoke to him before we met you yesterday.” He said between putting handfuls of gruel into his mouth. “He’s one of the third year dual mages, can’t remember his name though.”

After they had all finished, two people wearing the same robes that boy had worn, met them at the door to the main hall. They introduced themselves as the other two first year dual mages, Tobias, and Isla – the two Earth Water mages. They did not seem to be worried by Aaron, he smiled at them in gratitude. “Do you know why that guy wanted to see us?” Isla asked them. Everyone shook their heads and walked back to the common room and found the older dual mages sat in a group with five empty chairs ready for the new dual mage students.

As the first years got closer, the one that had spoken to them in the main hall noticed Aaron with the first year dual mages, after nervously looking around the seated group he stood up to get a sixth chair. He put it next to the empty chairs and sat back down.

“Let’s get straight to it.” He began, after the new arrivals had all sat down.

There were six fourth years, three third years and three second years. Making their group smaller than most of the groups sat in the common room, the only smaller one being the group of Healers.

“I’m Oliver, an Earth Water mage, as you can tell by my robes.” He introduced himself. “None of us really know when students started doing this, but it’s been done for as long as any of us have been here.” He gestured to thc rcst of the older students. “The day that we all first get here, yesterday for you. It always seems to be kind of a blur. It’s only when we try to go to sleep, that things start to get real.” He began, looking round the group of new students.

Aaron noticed that Oliver looked at everyone but him.

“At some point, a pretty clever student decided that those that have recently been through the same things should help the new students adjust. Kind of an unwritten rule.” He continued, still not looking at Aaron. “Every one of us has left a life behind, so if any of you want to talk about it, we know what it’s like.” He looked around the group again, again not looking at Aaron.

Aaron looked around at the other first years and noticed that they all looked a little worried, and reluctant to talk to this new group. He hadn’t thought too much about it, but because this Oliver refused to look at him, he decided to speak.

“To be honest, with everything that’s happened to me since I got here. And everyone staring or refusing to look at me.” He said pointedly. “I haven’t given it much thought, but I’m not leaving much behind. I didn’t have a girlfriend, or a boyfriend, no non gender specific partner. I never had children, found out when I was a teenager that I couldn’t have kids.” As he said that, he noticed his fellow first years nodding.

Aaron looked back to the older students and continued. “I didn’t have any brothers or sisters to leave behind and my parents both died years ago. I do kind of feel sorry for the taxi driver that I ‘died’ in front of though.” He looked around at everyone, the older students forcing themselves to look at him now that he had pointed it out. “I’m not really worried about being here. I was about to leave the Army after twenty four years, I had already said my goodbyes to most of the people that I knew.” He noticed some worried glances, but he carried on. “I didn’t know what I was going to do with my life, but now I’m here all I have to do is what I’m told and be where I’m told to be. It’s almost like being in the Army again.” He sighed and looked directly at Oliver. “I noticed your worried looks then. Yes, I was in the Army for twenty four years, but I spent most of that time, fighting against bullying. I can’t stand it, I can’t stand it when people treat people badly just because they are different, or because they don’t fit in with what is considered normal.”

Oliver nodded. “As far as I know, everyone here was an only child, and I don’t know if anyone had children.” He said, completely glossing over Aarons last point.

Aaron looked around the whole group and saw every one of them shaking their heads. He noticed Tala had her head bowed, not looking at anyone.

"I was in India. My parents were dead as well." Ajit began. "I was poor and always hungry, since I've been here, I've eaten more than I have in the last week." He said smiling. "I didn't have a girlfriend, could never seem to keep one. So, it was just me. And so far, if I'm being honest, it seems better here."

Aaron heard Tala sniffing, he reached over and laid his hand on hers. "Are you Ok?" He asked quietly.

"Who's going to feed my dog?" She asked looking up, tears streaming down her face. "I know it's ridiculous, but I didn't have anyone, and she was all I had."

"It's not ridiculous." Said one of the third year girls, an Air Fire mage by the robes she was wearing. "When I got here, I cried for weeks wondering who was going to look after my fish." She smiled at Tala. "What kind of dog is she?"

"She's a Pomeranian, I've had her since she was a puppy. I called her Floof." She chuckled as she gripped Aaron's hand.

They continued talking for a while, Tobias and Isla sharing the lives they had left behind on Earth. When they were finished everyone looked expectantly to Amelie, but she remained tight lipped and did not say a word.

When it was clear that she wasn't going to say anything, Oliver cleared his throat and spoke to the group again. "Ok, well, remember that we are around if you want to talk. Any of you." He looked around the older students, then looked directly at Aaron. "And we really do mean Any of you."

6

Aaron, Tala, Amelie, and Ajit were sat in the main hall with the rest of the newly arrived first year students after breakfast on Monday morning. They had waited while the timetables had been handed out to the rest of the school by the branch professors before the Head Mistress addressed them.

“Ok, if you could all separate to where your branch professors are, with the dual branch mages and the All-Power remaining in the centre of the hall.”

Tala, Amelie, Ajit, and Aaron walked to the centre of the hall to join the other two dual branch mage students, Isla and Tobias. Aaron looked around the hall to see the five professors handing out timetables to their new students and the Head Mistress approaching the group in the middle. She gave the dual mages their timetables before turning to Aaron, she held out his timetable but kept a vice like grip on it once he had taken hold of it.

“Mr Scott, please remain in the hall once everyone else has been dismissed.”

Aaron nodded and she let go of his timetable, she turned and moved back to the stage at the front of the hall. She glanced around the massive room to ensure everyone had been given their timetables before addressing the entire group.

"Your first two lessons will be in this hall, they are the only lessons you will receive as a year group. Every other lesson after these, you will be split into your branch groups. That is to say, the groups you are stood in right now." She smiled and looked at each separate group. "Before those lessons however, your branch professors will lead you on a tour of the school. Please return to this hall and be in your branch groups ready in one hours' time."

Aaron watched as the rest of the students left the hall and then turned back to the Head Mistress, she smiled at him as she walked towards a table with two chairs, she sat in the chair facing into the room and gestured to the empty seat.

"Take a seat, Mr Scott."

Aaron walked to the table, glancing behind him as he did. He saw the branch professors walking slowly across the hall towards the table. If he sat in that seat, he would not be able to see them or any attack coming from them, he picked the chair up and moved it to the side before sitting in a position that gave him a clear view of all the other people in the hall.

"Hmm. You are not a very trusting person, are you Mr Scott?" The head mistress said as he sat down.

"I am normally but given what's happened since I got here. I'm finding it difficult to trust anyone." He replied while warily looking between all of the professors.

The Head Mistress let out a sigh and smiled sadly. "Yes, we have been informed. Do not worry, Mr Lawson is being dealt with. That's Dylan, the boy who attacked you." She added as she noticed Aarons confused look. "Unlike schools on Earth however, we do not have the luxury of expelling a student. Every mage must be fully trained, or they would potentially be a danger to all those around them. I do not believe you need to worry about him at the moment though, it sounds as though what you did on Friday, with no magical training whatsoever, convinced him to not attempt anything like that again."

The rest of the professors reached them, picked up chairs and sat a few paces away from the table, with Aaron watching every move they made.

"But we are your professors, we are charged with your care while you are here at Doctrina. You need not fear us Mr Scott." The head mistress continued.

Aaron looked back to her. "Really?" He asked, once again sounding much more aggressive than he intended to. "So, the looks that all of you gave me when we found out I was an All-Power meant nothing?" He looked every professor in the eye as he asked. "You're not worried that I'm already a crazy villain that's going to start a war?"

"We are worried, Mr Scott." She answered honestly. "But not that you'll start a war, we are worried about your safety, the other student's safety, the safety of Doctrina and how we are going to teach you how to control your magic when none of us know the full extent of an All-Powers capabilities."

Aaron was taken aback by her honesty, he had expected her to say that they were not worried, her honesty impressed him.

“As you well know by now. There are some students here that would try to attack you to stop you from doing something in the future, the professors and I, fear that such attacks could inadvertently force you to withdraw into yourself. Therefore, harbouring ill feeling to all those that have attacked you, eventually causing you to snap and do the very thing that all your attackers feared you would do.” She looked to the professors. “Every student in this school will be informed of this, because as you so eloquently put it on Friday. They should get to know you before trying to kill you.” The professors all nodded in agreement. “Although, I would personally prefer it if none of my students tried to kill another.” It was now Aarons turn to nod in agreement. Once again, she smiled sadly at Aaron. “You should know however, that every mage on Nerium knows that an All-Power has arrived here at Doctrina. That the Prime Mage has demanded regular updates on your progress, your demeanour, behaviour and even any friends you make.”

Aaron shifted uncomfortably in his chair. “Great. It sounds as though this entire world has already decided that I am a threat.” He said to no one in particular.

"I would love to be able to argue that that is not the case, however, I am afraid I agree." The Head Mistress continued. "Therefore, it is up to us in this hall, all of us, to change their minds and convince them otherwise. Every new student at Doctrina has a file with a rough outline of their background on Earth, obviously I read yours as soon as I left this hall on Friday. You spent years convincing others to treat each other better. To accept one another. To stamp out bullying and harassment. I feel this is something you need to continue to do, first at this school. Then on a much, much larger scale." She considered Aaron for a moment. "I will be writing to the Prime Mage this evening, you should know that I will report everything as accurately as I see it, I will not attempt to sway his opinion in any way other than to pass on the truth. This, I believe will include Miss Ramos, Mr Shah, and Miss Durand?"

Aaron was confused for a moment. "If that is Tala, Ajit, and Amelie, yes. I haven't asked for their last names."

The Head Mistress nodded and continued. "It is comforting to see that you are making friends and not being ostracised. One more thing before the rest of the first year return to begin their school tour, aside from the history books and everything taught here. Professors have been told for centuries that all All-Powers disagree with almost everything taught in History of Nerium. Almost as though they know a different account of history. Having never taught an All-Power, I nor any professor currently at this school do not know if this is true. Do you have any idea why this would be the case?"

Aaron considered not saying anything. After all, the book had *for All-Power eyes only* written in the title, but then he remembered thinking how one sided and tailored to suit him it felt. "I think I do." He admitted with a sigh. "One of my books is called – *An accurate history of The All-Power – for All-Power eyes only*. I've only looked at two chapters of it. My own, which is just a heading, my name, and a number, 763, I'm guessing that's the year here on Nerium."

The Head Mistress nodded and gestured for him to carry on.

"And the chapter before it, Alexander Miller. It painted him as a very peaceful person that wanted to be left alone, saying he only ever acted out of self defence and was constantly searching for isolation. But the whole chapter felt a lot like propaganda and very tailored to me personally. I could show you if you like."

The Head Mistress shook her head. "As it says for All-Power eyes only, no one but an All-Power would be able to read it, to anyone else it would look to be nothing more than an empty notebook. How do you mean tailored to you?"

"I can't remember most of it, but it ended after Alexander had been stabbed in the back saying that – *Alexander Miller tried to relay to the Prime Mage that persecution and hatred was not the way, but he died before he could say more than "One day you will learn"*. I read that on Friday and haven't opened it since."

The Head Mistress looked thoughtful. “That is different from what you will learn later today, we will catch up again on Friday. Let me know your thoughts on the history subject then. But the other students are on their way back so we will end our conversation for today.”

Moments later the first of the students walked back into the hall. Tala, Amelie, and Ajit being among them, they saw Aaron and he set off towards them and they sat together towards the back of the hall. They immediately asked what the Head Mistress had wanted with him, and he filled them in.

“That’s big, sounds like the whole world is against you already.” Ajit said when Aaron had finished.

Aaron looked at him and the other two. “Not just me, the three of you as well if you stay my friends...”

“Don’t you dare say another word.” Amelie interrupted him, shaking her head. “We aren’t going anywhere, we are going to help you change everyone’s mind. Taylors right, if we just carry on like normal and just learn like normal students then everyone will see that you’re just a normal person that’s been thrown into this craziness.”

Tala laid her hand on Aarons. “And if anyone wants to attack you, we’ll be there with you. But from everything we’ve heard, you won’t really need any help.” She moved her hand away and added as an afterthought. “Do you think she’s right? About the book? That only you can read it.”

Aaron had not considered that the Head Mistress might be wrong. But before he could mention it again, they were joined by Isla and Tobias. The two smiled as they sat near them, and they all waited for their professors to arrive to give them a tour.

They watched as the Earth mages left with Professor Hawthorn, a few minutes later Professor Fray led the Air mages away, then the Water mages left with Professor Quail, Professor Gibson took the Fire mages after them and finally Professor Iaso led the Healers out of the hall.

The six of them sat there for a moment wondering if they had been forgotten about, when two new professors, each wearing the same dual mage robes as the new dual mages sat waiting for them, walked into the hall.
"Good morning everyone, I am Professor Flak, your Air Fire dual professor." The shorter one with blindingly bright white hair introduced herself smiling at the six first years.

"And I'm Professor Loam, your Earth Water dual professor." The other introduced herself, in stark contrast to Professor Flaks blindingly bright white hair, Professor Loam had long hair so dark that it seemed to swallow all the light around it.

"Follow along and we'll show you around the school." Professor Flak said as the new dual mages and Aaron stood to follow them. "As dual mages, you are the lucky ones here at Doctrina, class sizes are always much, much smaller."

“Indeed, Miss Kelly and Mr Fleck, the two of you have the smallest class size in the year, we will of course be joined occasionally by Mr Scott.” Professor Loam smiled at Aaron. “Mr Scott, you have my personal apologies, I am afraid you will be passed around from professor to professor. The rest of you will spend most of your time with Professor Flak.” She said as the two of them led the group out of the main hall.

The students followed their new professors around the ground floor, the walls were all made from extremely smooth black stone, the windows were small, and the lighting came from smokeless flaming torches.

There were classrooms for the Earth mages, numbered one to three, and Water mage classrooms, again, numbered one to three. One room for each year group. There were also four classrooms for Earth Water dual mages, each numbered on the door.

“This one will be the classroom that we will be using this year Miss Kelly, Mr Fleck and Mr Scott.” Professor Loam said as they reached a door with a large number one on it.

The final classroom on the ground floor was for the rarest dual branch, the Water Fire dual classroom. The professors stopped at the bottom of a set of stairs and by a door at the end of the corridor.

“You will see these doors on each of the floors, beyond these are the professors’ offices. An office for each of the professors that have classrooms on the floor.” Professor Flak took over as she led the group up to the first floor.

This floor had three Fire mage classrooms and three Healer classrooms, each numbered one to three. "Mr Scott, you will be learning in this room this year." Professor Flak added as they passed Healing classroom one.

The last room on the first floor was the History of Nerium classroom. "Professor Horton teaches the dual mages in his office as the class is much smaller. His office, unlike every other professor, is right next to his classroom." Professor Loam said as they reached the stairs to the second floor.

On the second and top floor of the school there were three Air mage classrooms, four Air Fire dual classrooms and one Earth Air classroom for the second rarest dual branch.

Professor Flak stopped outside Air Fire Classroom one. "Air Fire mages and Mr Scott, this is where we will be learning this year." She opened the door and ushered them all inside.

Air Fire Classroom one was a room as large as the main hall with one major difference, this classroom had no ceiling. The professor noticed the first years looking up to the open sky above them. "Yes. In a few months we will be experimenting with flight."

Every head whipped round to her, Aaron noticed that Isla and Tobias looked slightly disheartened as they would not be learning to fly.

Professor Flak smiled. “Yes, you heard correctly, I said flight. But, for now we will be staying firmly on the ground.” She smiled at them all. “As all the classrooms on this floor are used by mages with Air abilities, thcy are all roofless. Are there any questions about the tour?”

“Yes professor.” Aaron said, he had noticed a large tower rising into the sky from the corner of the classroom. “What’s in there?” He said pointing towards it.

“That, Mr Scott. Is a very good question. That is called Lock tower, please don’t ask us why it is called that, all anyone knows is that it was named such by the schools’ builder.” Professor Loam answered. “Since the school was built, professors and students alike have searched for a way in, there does not seem to be any doors or hatches leading inside.”

“And there are no windows for flyers to enter through either, the roof is just as inaccessible.” Professor Flak added. “Fire mages have attempted to burn their way in, but the tower remained undamaged.”

“Similarly, Earth mages have attempted to gain access through vibrating the stone and growing vines in-between the separate stones, to no avail.” Professor Loam continued. “And there are flowing rivers in each of the Water mage classrooms that run against the base of the tower, after over seven hundred years the tower shows no sign of erosion.”

7

“I’d like you three to try to read my book with me, if that’s ok.” Aaron said once they were sat in the main hall waiting for their first lesson to begin. They agreed without much thought. “You’ve all been hoping I’d say that, haven’t you?” He added with a smile.

“Of course we have.” Replied Ajit with a smile of his own. “You can’t tell us you have a history book that’s different to what we’re being taught and expect us not to want to read it.”

“It’s not just a different history.” Amelie joined in. “This is a completely different world, we know nothing about this place except for what these professors tell us. It might be that neither version of history is the complete truth, it might be that each version has parts of the truth. But it could also mean that one is a complete lie. The only way to find out is to learn as much as we can from every possible source.”

Their conversation was cut short as a professor walked in, through the seated students and to the front of the hall.

“Good morning, welcome to Nerium and Doctrina school.” He said quietly yet every single person in the room heard him as though he was sat right next to them. He was a tall, very thin, very old Air mage. “I am Professor Horton; I have been teaching History of Nerium for a very long time.”

Aaron was sure that everyone believed him, he looked as though he had lived through all of Neriums history.

“This first lesson will be about Nerium itself.” The professor continued as he took a seat at the front of the hall. “On Nerium, the days are the same length, and we measure time the same way we did on Earth, we use the same days and months, the only difference is that, here on Nerium the years are marked by the arrival of the new mages. Those being yourselves.” He held out his arms in a welcoming gesture and smiled at the room. “This happens, without fail every ten months, meaning that a year here lasts only ten months. The months are named the same as they are on Earth with the exception of February and November, those two months do not exist here. A year on Nerium is forty four weeks or three hundred and six days.” He paused to take a drink. “The years have been counted since the first humans arrived on this world. The year we are currently in is 763. Meaning of course that humans have been transported to Nerium for the last seven hundred and sixty three years. Many historians and theologians have asked the question of how this happened, how we were first brought here, or indeed, why we have been brought to Nerium. We have yet to find an answer.” The professor stood and walked in a large circle on the stage at the front of the hall. “Before the age of students was changed, this next bit of information used to elicit a much larger reaction.”

He paused again and Aaron could tell that whatever he was about to say was something he did not enjoy teaching.

"You may or may not have noticed that each student here in this room. You, being the entire first year. Has been brought from Earth, there is not a single student in this school that was born on Nerium." He paused to take a breath again. "That is because, there has not been a single birth on Nerium for the entire time that humans have inhabited it. Not one person brought here has been able to sire or carry a child." He stopped as though waiting for the hall to erupt with complaints.

Aaron looked around and saw quite a few other people looking around, none of them looked angry or upset.

When no complaints came, the professor continued. "When I was a student, we were brought here when we were sixteen, and a lot of us were quite angry when we heard that, even after all this time it still stings a little." He stopped pacing and sat back down. "But, like I said, since the age was changed, it seems that not one person brought here has had children while they were on Earth. It also seems that many already knew that they were unable to have children. This, it is believed, is also the reason why you look like teenagers. You are the youth of Nerium, you are Neriums future." He smiled into the room again. "Moving on to holidays and such, birthdays are not celebrated as they are on Earth. As everyone has the same birthday, January 1st, that being the day that every one of us arrived here, and seeing as we were all brought here from Earth on our birthdays, that makes January 1st all of our birthdays. This is probably the last time you will hear these words, Happy belated Birthday." He smiled to the seated students.

"We do not throw individual parties or give gifts, however in every village and town there are feasts and a celebration of life held every year. There are three more celebrations of life held throughout the year, these are held at the end of each season, the end of spring, the end of summer and the end of autumn." He looked around the room waiting for questions, none came so he continued. "Like the months of February and November, winter does not exist here. You will know when they arrive as you will have a two week break in learning for each. The autumn celebrations being held, coincidentally, on the 25th of December."

The professor went on to talk about the terrain of Nerium, it sounded a lot like Earth to Aaron so he zoned out, he would learn about the terrain himself.

After lunch they were back in the main hall waiting for Professor Horton and their next history lesson, Aaron found himself getting impatient. He wanted to see if he could do any magic, he didn't want history lessons. Especially if they were like the history in his All-Power book.

"In this lesson, your second history lesson of the day. Don't worry, this is the only time that will happen." Professor Horton began as he re-entered the hall, almost as though he knew that everyone was tired of listening to him talk about Nerium already. "I will teach you about the last war on Nerium. Let us hope it remains the last war." He said pointedly. "The year was 587 and the last All-Power, until now." A lot of students turned to look at Aaron, Aaron ignored them all. "Was a man named Alexander Miller."

Aaron already knew this but was very interested in hearing what differences this version of history had to his book.

“Now, Miller had been a student here in this very school until the year 531, but nothing is known about what he did or where he went for the years between completing his studies here and his return in the year 587.”

That’s because he was trying to stay isolated away from everyone, Aaron found himself thinking.

“He returned in rather a dramatic way.” The professor continued. “He appeared in a town called Senin with the lifeless bodies of seven young mages. He gave no explanation as to who they were, nor why he had killed them. Instead, he stated to the populous of the town that, and these were his words ‘More is to come’.”

The book did say that the people of the town had refused to listen to him, Aaron thought.

“And once again Miller vanished. The Prime Mage of the time was informed, and he dispatched ten of his mages to apprehend Miller. The next thing anyone knew, all ten were dead and Miller was nowhere to be found.”

Aaron nodded to himself, so far there isn’t much difference in the events apart from the perspective, he continued his analysis.

"The Prime Mage set a reward for Millers capture, but he was not sighted for another three months. Miller reappeared three hundred miles away close to another town, once again ten mages were sent to bring him in. This time however, Miller did not flee after killing the mages, instead he paraded their bodies into the town. He used a form of magic unknown to any other mage to incapacitate an elderly farmer and forced him to watch as the entire town was slaughtered. Miller then sent the farmer to the Prime Mage with a message. *'Their blood is on your hands.'* That was Millers message to the Prime Mage."

Ok that's different, Aaron thought. He was so glued to every word coming from Professor Horton that he had not noticed more and more faces turning to look at him.

"More and more mages were sent to apprehend Miller over the next twenty six years, always with the same result. The mages would be slain along with the inhabitants of the closest town, leaving one survivor to pass on the same message. Miller would not listen to reason. In the year 613, Miller arrived in Statera to storm the Imperium houses to overthrow the Prime Mage and claim power for himself. Seventy mages were in attendance on that day, including the Prime Mage. Miller slaughtered fifty seven mages before a lone mage managed to get behind him and finally bring him down. With his dying breath Miller uttered one final threat. '*One day you will learn'*. Six thousand and seventy nine mages lost their lives during the twenty six year war against one All-Power. Something that no living mage wants to see again." With those last words Professor Horton looked directly at Aaron.

Professor Horton instructed everyone to open their textbooks and for the next forty minutes he led them through various towns and villages that were decimated during the twenty six year war against Alexander Miller.

By the time the lesson had finished Aaron was only sure of one thing – this textbook went into a lot more detail than his All-Power book, he was still hoping that despite everything written in the textbook that there had to be some truths in both of the books.

8

"Are you with us for the next session?" Tala asked, breaking into Aaron's thoughts.

He hadn't even looked at his timetable yet, he quickly pulled it out to look.

Week One

Monday

1. School tour
2. History of Nerium – Main Hall
3. Lunch
4. History of Nerium. – Main Hall required; *Wars of Nerium – working back through time.*
5. Air Fire dual – Air Fire Classroom one

He told Tala that he was, and quickly scanned through the rest of the week.

Tuesday

1. Earth Water dual – Earth Water Classroom one
2. Earth Air dual – Earth Air Classroom
3. Lunch
4. Water Fire dual – Water Fire Classroom
5. Air Fire dual – Air Fire Classroom one

Wednesday

1. Earth Water dual – Earth Water Classroom one
2. Earth Air dual – Earth Air Classroom
3. Lunch
4. Water Fire dual - Water Fire Classroom

5. History of Nerium – Main hall - required; *Wars of Nerium – working back through time.*

Thursday

1. Healing – Healing classroom one
2. Air Fire dual – Air Fire Classroom one
3. Lunch
4. Earth Water dual – Earth Water Classroom one
5. Earth Air dual – Earth Air Classroom

Friday

1. Water Fire – Water Fire Classroom
2. All-Power self-study
3. Lunch
4. History of Nerium – Professor Hortons office - required; *Wars of Nerium – working back through time.*
5. Meeting with Head Mistress Taylor, Head Mistress' office.

Aaron and the four Air Fire mages were in Air Fire Classroom one with Professor Flak for their final lesson of their first day.

"To start, let me make sure I have you all right. Mr Scott, I know who you are, you'll get that quite a lot, I'm afraid every professor has read your file and knows who you are, and it isn't as though you could hide wearing those robes either. As I'm sure you have guessed we have to monitor and report back to the head mistress." She smiled sympathetically.

Aaron nodded. "Head Mistress Taylor told me, yeah."

She smiled and continued, pointing to each of them as she said a name. “I would apologise for making assumptions, but I’ve been doing this quite a while and I’ve rarely been wrong. Miss Ramos, Filipino name, that would make you Miss Durand. And you must be Mr Shah.” She nodded as if congratulating herself for guessing correctly and continued. “Unlike schools on Earth, there is no curriculum here at Doctrina. This, most of us believe to be a good thing, as it means we can cater each lesson to your advantage. There are no exams at Doctrina, we teach you until both professor and student are happy that they can control their own branch of magic, in your cases, multiple branches. All dual mages and, as far as I am aware, every All-Power remains at Doctrina for four years. As Professor Loam alluded to earlier, I will teach you throughout your entire learning journey. Each year group has different professors, meaning that the dual mages in their second, third and fourth years each have their own professor that solely teaches them. Mr Scott, you will have quite a few separate professors teaching you.” Once again, she smiled sadly at Aaron. “But, the professors that will teach you this year, will teach you for your entire school journey.” She turned back to address the whole group. “Like I said, we can cater each lesson to your advantage. As yet I do not know your strengths or weaknesses, nor do you. However, this lesson will certainly be to your advantage.” She looked directly at Aaron. “Given what happened on Friday.”

Professor Flak told the group how to harden the air around them to form a shield which, if the mage was strong enough, would be enough to deflect almost any attack.

Aaron fought the feeling of ridiculousness as he began to search within him for the source of his Air magic, as Professor Flak had instructed him. It only took him a few minutes of feeling silly before he found what he was looking for. A feeling of lightness around the outside of his chest, around his ribs and his lungs. Once he had found it, he moved on to what the professor had said to do next, he concentrated hard on pushing that feeling out so that it first filled his body, then beyond to fill the air around him.

Professor Flak hid a look of shock as she saw this, clearly the professor was able to see the changes in the air.

“Excellent work Mr Scott, now feel through the air and concentrate on hardening it.”

Aaron was not sure how to do that, but he imagined the bubble of air he had just created around him being as hard as concrete. After another few minutes he began to feel his air bubble harden to form a shield.

For the next hour they practiced shielding while Professor Flak tested their shields with light fire bursts, by the time the class was finished Aarons’ shield was near enough impenetrable.

“Excellent work today, with enough practice you could be able to keep your shields up every waking minute.” The professor beamed as she dismissed the class.

Aaron had agreed with Amelie, Tala, and Ajit to check the All-Power book that evening and that it would be best to read it in private, he had been expecting the four of them to enter his room after dinner and they would start trying to read the book straight away. One look at their faces when they walked into his room, and he knew that that was not going to be the case.

The three of them walked through the library, the bedroom, the bathroom and back again.

"This is insane! Its bigger than my house back on Earth." Tala announced.

"Why aren't our rooms like this?" Ajit blurted out.

"That bath is like a swimming pool!" Amelie said, her stunned look mirroring the look on the faces of the other two.

Aaron was a little taken aback, he had assumed everyone's rooms were the same. "Aren't your rooms like this? What are your rooms like?"

Tala answered. "Well, me and Amelie share a room the same size as this library. We have single beds, not like the gigantic bed you have. We have a small desk and a shelf with about twenty books each." The stunned look still on her face. "Oh, and we have a really uncomfortable chair each too. Not a sofa and an armchair in our own private library."

"Not to mention the fact that our desks are less than half the size of your desk. Or, that we have communal bathrooms." Ajit jumped in. "Male and Female, we don't all share the same one, which isn't too bad for me because I kind of get my own bathroom. It's nowhere near as nice as yours though."

"Clearly the school isn't afraid of you, or at least whoever built the school." Amelie said as she sank into the sofa. "Do we know who did build this school?" She added almost to herself.

"I think that's a question for another time." Aaron answered, sitting in the armchair. "Right now, shall we focus on the question of the book." He said as he held up *An accurate history of The All-Power* with the cover facing them.

"Is that it?" Tala asked as she and Ajit joined Amelie on the sofa.

"That's what the cover says." Aaron replied as he pointed to the title. All three of them shook their head. "You can't even see the title?"

"It's just a blank cover." Tala said as she held out a hand for the book.

Aaron got up and gave it to her, then he moved around behind the sofa, so that he could see the pages as Tala leafed through them. As she did, he could see all the writing was still there. "Do you see it?"

"No, nothing. It looks just like a really old empty book to me." Ajit replied, shaking his head as the other two nodded in agreement.

Aaron took the book back from Tala and sat in the armchair again. "OK then, looks like it's story time." He joked as he found the start of Alexander Millers chapter.

"Well, that's definitely different from what the old professor told us this morning." Amelie said after Aaron had finished reading. "It looks like there's quite a few pages left after Miller, what else is in there?"

"There's a load of blank pages then the start of the next chapter, but it only has…" Aaron stopped as he turned the pages and saw more than just his name. "That's not possible. I haven't opened this book since Friday and all that was on this page was my name and this year. Now there's a whole new page." He said looking up at the other three.

Tala laughed. "We are all forty two, in our sixteen year old bodies, we are on a different planet, we are learning magic and today we found out that we are going to learn how to fly. But a book writing itself is where you draw the line? What does the new page say?"

Aaron frowned sarcastically at her. "Don't you come at me with that logic." He laughed back at her as he looked back down to the page and began to read aloud.

"Aaron Scott 763 –

From the moment of Aaron Scott's arrival at Doctrina he faced the paranoia of the professors and immediately knew he was special.

Within an hour of meeting the other students at Doctrina he survived an unprovoked attack on his life by absorbing a burst of flame hot enough to melt glass, showing his raw magical talent from the very start.

That very day he also did something that no other All-Power had ever managed before him – he gained a following, impressed by his power, three Dual Mages pledged their allegiance to him."

Aaron looked up at the other three. "When did you pledge your allegiance to me?" He said, only half-jokingly.

"We didn't, we're your friends not your followers. Is that all it says?" Amelie answered.

Aaron shook his head and continued.

"The Prime Mage of the time – Prime Mage Reid ordered surveillance on Aaron Scott, the moment he learnt of the emergence of a new All-Power.

However, Doctrina's head mistress, Head Mistress Taylor warned Aaron Scott of this allowing him to intentionally cater what others saw of him, therefore giving him control of what the Prime Mage heard of him.

On his very first day of learning at Doctrina Aaron Scott displayed how powerful he would become by learning what takes other students, including other All-Powers, weeks if not months.

That's it, so far." Aaron said as he finished reading. "There are a few truths in there, I noticed the looks on the professors faces, I was attacked, and the Prime Mage has ordered surveillance." He shook his head as he thought more. "But it's twisting things, like you all being my followers, the strength of Dylan's attack, me catering what people see and me displaying how powerful I would become." He looked up at the other three. "We've only had one magic lesson. This book is weird." He shook his head as he looked through the page again.

"Does the book have an author on it?" Amelie asked, breaking Aaron away from the page.

Aaron hadn't even thought to look, he checked the cover and then the first pages. "No, nothing." He said quietly, he threw the pages over to look at the back page. Then he saw it, flowing handwritten letters at the bottom centre of the very last page. "Oh wait, it's here.

Originally created by Isabella Lockton with contributions from all following All-Powers for all All-Powers to come.

We the All-Powers are here to rule.

Never forget."

"Isabella Lockton. Ok, we can ask the professors to see what they know about her." Amelie said almost to herself.

Aaron shook his head as he moved back to the start of the book. “No need for that, she’s in here. She was the first All-Power. I haven’t read her chapter, but there’s a small piece about her before the contents page. Where is it? Ah, here we go.

When humans first appeared on Nerium there was an All-Power.

The first All-Power.

Isabella Lockton, all the lesser mages grew to fear her, simply because she was more than them.

She made a prophecy, the only prophecy ever made in Neriums recorded history.

‘There will be an All-Power that will rule Nerium for eternity, they will teach this world the meaning of fear.’

It has never been clear whether this is a true prophecy or the angry words of a persecuted All-Power.”

“Why haven’t you read her chapter?” Ajit asked, he looked at Amelie and Tala. “If I was in your shoes, I’d have read that whole book cover to cover.” Again, he looked to the other two on the sofa. “I mean, don’t you want to know everything you can?”

Aaron gave him a small smile. “On Friday, after Dylan tried to do me in. I already didn’t want to believe that every All-Power was bad or evil. I came in here and I read Alexander Millers chapter and it freaked me out. That’s when I went out to the tree and met the three of you. Then, after what the head mistress said about All-Powers disagreeing with everything taught about All-Power war history, I decided not to read more chapters until after a history lesson.”

Ajit and Amelie nodded like they understood but Tala looked thoughtful. “Your chapter in the book, what did it say about you, the head mistress and the Prime Mage?” Confused, Aaron flipped back to his chapter and found the part she meant. “It says,

The Prime Mage of the time – Prime Mage Reid ordered surveillance on Aaron Scott, the moment he learnt of the emergence of a new All-Power.

However, Doctrina’s head mistress, Head Mistress Taylor warned Aaron Scott of this allowing him to intentionally cater what others saw of him therefore giving him control of what the Prime Mage heard of him.

Why?”

She looked nervous for a moment. “Please don’t take this the wrong way but that’s another truth, its twisting it to make it sound like you’re doing it on purpose. But, by not reading the chapters until after each lesson you won’t have anything to disagree with. And, by not disagreeing, you’re making sure that the Prime finds out that you’re behaving differently than every All-Power they know about.”

When Amelie, Ajit and Tala had left, Aaron was not tired, so he picked up another book, the smallest book on his All-Power shelf.

Notable All-Power abilities uncommon in other Mages

Aaron read for the next thirty minutes not able to believe that he could have these abilities. There was no way he could plant thoughts in peoples head with just a look (noted in Henry Carmine), or cause someone to burst into flames with a click of his fingers (noted in Anastasia Solovyov), and there was absolutely no way he could rip all the liquid from a person's body leaving them desiccated and definitely dead (noted in Isabella Lockton).

He put the book down and paced his room for a while before deciding to practice his Air shield, as he felt the air harden around him, he wondered what would happen if he tried to harden the air under his feet as well. He closed his eyes and concentrated but didn't feel any change, he gave up after a few minutes and opened his eyes, that's when he saw that he was stood on solid air a foot above the ground. He let out a half excited, half terrified laugh and fell back down to the ground. For the next hour he practiced this, until he could glide around his room by just thinking.

He smiled to himself, magic was coming easily to him, maybe the book was right about him. Maybe he was special.

9

The next day Aaron discovered that Professor Loam had done something very similar to Professor Flak. As Tobias and Isla continued their practice, the professor told Aaron how to raise the earth in front of him to form a wall like shield.

Aaron searched within himself as he had done the day before in his Air Fire class, this time he found the source of his Earth magic in the soles of his feet, a heavy solid feeling. He concentrated on pushing that feeling down and into the ground beneath him.

Almost instantly, the ground near to him began to feel like an extension of his own body. He thought hard about raising the ground in front of him. Slowly, the ground tore apart, like a blanket folding back on itself, and lifted in front of him.

By the time the lesson was finished Aaron could produce an Earth shield better than either Tobias or Isla could, this earned him praise and a worried look from Professor Loam.

Aaron's other dual classes continued the same way they had started, Professor Turner the Earth Air dual professor, his robes were dark green on the bottom and sky blue on the top, took what Aaron had learnt from Professor Loam and Professor Flak and merged the two together.

"Instead of lifting the ground to form a wall in front of you." He had begun. "What you will do now, is break the ground into chunks. Then attach them to your Air shield." He demonstrated as he spoke. Aaron watched as the professor lifted pieces of the ground and set them swirling around him.

"I don't know how to make wind to fly the chunks of earth around me though, professor." Aaron said once Professor Turner had returned the chunks of earth back to the ground.

The professor shook his head and smiled at Aaron. "We are not using wind for this. Feel through your Air shield and connect the chunks to its exterior. All while spinning the surface of the shield. I do agree, however. It does look like wind is carrying the pieces around you." He said, still smiling.

Once more, Aaron was unsure how to connect the pieces of the ground to his Air shield, but he tried anyway. He raised his Air shield and imagined it spinning around him. He stumbled and dropped his shield, feeling suddenly dizzy.

The professor smiled at him again. "Best to start spinning it slowly until you get used to the sensation."

Aaron began again, this time spinning his shield slower. He sent his Earth magic into the ground and imagined it breaking into smaller rocks and bits of rubble, he smiled as he saw it begin to break apart. Then he imagined that the spinning surface of his Air shield was sticky, like glue. To his surprise, the rocks and rubble began to cling to it. By the end of his lesson Aaron was able to move rocks and earth around him so fast that not one of the professor's test spells could get through.

The Water Fire dual professor, his robes were blood red and deep blue split diagonally, Professor Stein was the first professor not to look at Aaron with either a worried or scared look on his face. He was just happy that he finally had a student to teach as the Water Fire combination was the rarest of the dual mages.

Aaron found that the source of his Water magic was in his mouth, and with some difficulty, he managed to draw moisture from the air around him. Next, he searched for the source of his Fire magic. He found this was within his heart. Using the two sources Aaron pulled the moisture from the air around him to form a sphere of liquid, then he used the source of his Fire magic to pull all of the heat from the liquid, forming an almost indestructible ice shield around him.

When the lesson was finished Aaron decided to ask a question that had been bothering him since he read the new page about himself. "Professor, can I ask you something?"

“You just did.” Professor Stein answered, laughing at his own joke. “But you can ask me anything, and please, don’t ask permission to ask if you can, before you do.”

“Ok. You’re the first professor here that hasn’t looked scared or worried after a lesson. How long does it normally take people to learn these shields?”

Professor Stein nodded with a small smile on his face. “Well, as I obviously don’t teach other lessons, I can’t speak for how long it takes young mages to learn the other shields. Although I have heard you are doing exceptionally well. But, for this ice shield.” He looked thoughtful for a moment, as though he was trying to decide whether he should continue or not. “What you have just learnt in one hour, took me almost three months to learn. If you are performing this well in your other lessons, I can see why the other professors may be worried.” He said honestly. “What you must understand however, is that every single mage that comes through this school. Which is to say, every mage on Nerium. Has learnt that every All-Power has murdered thousands of people each, and unfortunately there are quite a lot of mages that believe that just because you are an All-Power, that you will be the same. From what we have all heard and seen of you so far, I am choosing to believe that you won’t.” He smiled kindly at Aaron. “I like to believe that people aren’t good or bad, but that they are made one way or the other by their environment. If we, your professors, do what we can to make sure the other students don’t try to kill you.” He looked at Aaron. “Again.” He said, still smiling.

“And we make sure you stay out of trouble. The rest of the world might just see that you are a normal, albeit powerful mage. Hopefully that way we can change their minds about you.” He continued as he rocked back and forth on his heels. “Please remember that I am around, that I will be honest with you and that I will do my very best to not be worried by you.” He started laughing and added jokingly. “That way, if I’m wrong, and you do go bad. Just remember I was one of the good ones. You’d better head off for your next lesson.”

Aaron slowly left the classroom and walked up to the top floor, not sure what to make of Professor Steins last comment.

When he walked into Air Fire Classroom one, he walked over to where Tala, Amelie and Ajit were sitting, enjoying the sun during their break.

“You ok?” Tala asked. Aaron explained what had just happened as he sat down next to her. “Yeah, we thought something like that might happen.” She nodded when he had finished.

“But we didn’t expect anyone to come right out and say it though.” Amelie continued. “Even if he was trying to make a joke out of it. And before you even think about it, no. That’s not what we’re doing.”

“I wasn’t thinking that. I am now.” Aaron chuckled then shook his head. “I hadn’t thought anyone would be like that. How come you have?”

“I haven’t been thinking it.” Ajit joined in. “Any of it.”

"OK fine, me and Amelie have thought about it." Tala added. Aaron and Ajit looked between her and Amelie. "We share a room remember. We thought we'd have to keep an eye out for people like that but didn't think it would happen for a few weeks, and that they'd be more subtle about it."

Aaron looked between the two girls. "Alright, I'm not going to lie. I'm kind of happy that you two are thinking about things like that but surely you could find better things to talk about before bed."

"What would you like us to talk about? Boys?" Amelie said and stopped suddenly when Tala elbowed her in the chest. "We might look like teenage girls, but we're not." She finished with a glare at Tala.

Aaron glanced at Ajit who had laid back on the ground and had closed his eyes to enjoy the sun, he was paying no attention, completely oblivious to the conversation. He looked away from Ajit and smiled to himself but decided to let it go, for now. "Ok, ok, well next time you two have a night-time brainstorming session how about you let us two know about it as well?"

Professor Flak entered the room and instructed the dual mages to continue practicing and then looked to Aaron. "Welcome back Mr Scott, have you been practicing?" Aaron looked a little uneasy. "Is everything ok?"

“Are you, and the other professors… er… concerned with how fast I’m picking things up?” He asked not wanting to keep things hidden or ‘cater’ what others see.

“A little.” She admitted. “Please understand tha..”

“I know, I know.” Aaron interrupted. “Every mage on Nerium has been taught that all All-Powers are evil.”
“Yes, there is that, and there is only one professor here that was even on Nerium the last time an All-Power was alive, and he was a first year then. We have all heard stories about how powerful All-Powers are, but never witnessed it, until now.” She smiled tightly. “The speed at which you are learning is beyond impressive Mr Scott, and yes, I will admit that the years of being taught that All-Powers are, like you said, evil, have left a mark. But please believe me, none of the professors here are looking for signs that you are going bad.” She tried to smile at him. “So, have you been practicing?”

Aaron nodded. “Yeah, and I think I figured out how to fly.”

Professor Flak tilted her head and looked confused. “I’m not certain how you could get to flying from shields. Could you show me?”

Aaron nodded and almost effortlessly created an air shield around him, extending it beneath his feet which lifted him a foot above the ground, the professor put her hand to her mouth in shock.

“Mr Scott you are not flying.” Tala, Ajit, and Amelie noticed Aaron floating above the ground and stopped practicing to watch. “What you are doing is creating a shield so complete and so perfect, it is completely surrounding you.” The professor bent as if inspecting his shield. “I must say Mr Scott, in all my years here at Doctrina. I have never seen a shield so complete.”

“I’m sorry professor, but if I’m not flying. How can I move around?” He asked as he started gliding around the classroom.

Professor Flaks eyes looked as though they were about to pop right out of her head. “This is incredible.” She said as she followed him around the room. “The nearest I can guess is that you are creating a perfect sphere of a shield around you, and you are rolling that shield to carry you around. But, like I said, it’s a guess. I have never seen this, from anyone.” She shook her head. “Incredible.” The professor took a moment to compose herself. “OK then, clearly you don’t need to practice shields anymore. Why don’t you finish early and have an extra self-study session, I will work on a separate lesson plan for you for our next class.”

Aaron turned to leave the classroom and he saw Tala stood in front of the door staring at him with her arms folded.

“What you literally just said.” She began angrily when he got to her. “About Amelie and me sharing our brainstorming with you two.” She raised her eyebrows at him. “How about you do the same when you learn to do something amazing.” It was not a question.

Aaron looked down at her and smiled softly. “Yes Ma’am.”

“That’s better.” She smiled and blushed a little. “We’ll see you at dinner.”

The next day, his professors all tested his shields and every one of them decided they were good enough for him to move on. Professor Loam moved on to teach him how to deflect Earth attacks while Isla and Tobias practiced their shields, the professor pulled earth from the ground and shot it at him as he attempted to divert it back into the ground. Professor Turner did the same with air attacks, shooting strong wind at Aaron as he tried to disperse the wind.

Professor Stein worked on an ability that Aaron had already shown, he shot jets of fire at Aaron, so that he could perfect his ability to absorb the attack as he had already done without knowing how to, when Dylan had attacked him. The professor, however, made sure that the flames were cool enough not to do any damage to Aaron.

10

Aaron was sat with all five of the dual mages, they were waiting in the main hall for their next History of Nerium lesson when they heard Professor Horton as though he was sat with them. "Good afternoon everyone, please follow me." They all looked around to find him and saw that he was stood by the door. "Come along." And he turned and walked out of the hall.

The Professor led them up to the first floor and into his office next to the main History of Nerium classroom, the room had a desk for the professor, ten armchairs in a circle and there were so many paintings that there was hardly any wall left showing. "Take a seat everyone." Professor Horton said as he sat behind the desk and let out a sigh. "Teaching the Healers and you dual mages is always my favourite, there are always so few of you that I can teach you, here in my office." He said with a smile. "Before we get started with lesson two, does anyone have any questions from your first lesson?"

Aaron had a question but not about the last lesson, so he chose to wait until after the lesson to ask it.

Amelie had one to ask though. "Actually, yes professor. You said that Alexander Miller disappeared between the years 531 to 587, what do you think he was doing in those years?"

He gave her an impressed look. "Not a question that has been asked before, I like that kind of question." He nodded with a smile. "But, I have given it quite a bit of thought, you see, when he was here at Doctrina he never attacked or hurt anyone. Although he was attacked many times himself, by the professors as well as the students, he only ever acted out of self-preservation and defended himself. As I said in the last lesson, nothing is known about what he did or where he went, but my guess. And it is an educated guess, is that he wanted to be left alone and then something happened. Something happened which changed his desire for solitude, and the events of the last lesson unfolded. Does that answer your question?" Amelie nodded and thanked him, there were no more questions, so he began. "Does anyone know the name of the All-Power that arrived on Nerium, before Alexander Miller?" With that question he looked directly at Aaron.

Aaron smiled and nodded. "It was Henry Carmine. That's all I know about him."

"That is correct Mr Scott, Henry Carmine is the next most recent All-Power." He said with an approving nod. "Now with Henry Carmine, there is no missing time and no need for educated guesses. Like Alexander Miller, he was attacked many times while he was at school, but unlike Miller, he did not act out of defence, with every attack he fought back sending each and every one of his attackers to be treated by the Healers. He did stop short of killing anyone while he was here, but that was the only way in which he showed restraint. He constantly pushed his abilities, sometimes to the point of injuring himself."

Professor Horton began almost absentmindedly as he shuffled papers on his desk. "He did this so many times that his ability to heal himself became almost a natural response. Once, in an attempt to perfect one of his abilities, he burst blood vessels in his brain, and if he were not so well practiced in healing himself, he could well have died. So here we are, Henry Carmine hasn't even left Doctrina yet and he is already powerful enough to heal himself even when his brain is damaged, he is also not concerned about whether or not he hurts people who attack him." He paused so that the dual mages and Aaron could take that information in. "After completing his studies here, Carmine went straight to the Imperium houses, that is the main government building on Nerium located in the only city in human populated Nerium, Statera. Small side note, Imperium is Latin for government, just as Doctrina is Latin for learning." He smiled at the group. "But back to Henry Carmine, he went to the Imperium houses in search of work, which he got. He was offered a low-level position which he accepted, and he worked hard for three years constantly pushing for promotion throughout, which he did not get. He scheduled a meeting with Prime Mage Garcia, as an All-Power working in government the two had regular meetings. But this meeting was to be their last, Carmine decapitated him. As the two were alone in the Prime Mages office we do not know how, but what we do know is that Carmine paraded the Primes head and body through the halls and declared himself the new Prime Mage. Obviously, the mages in the halls tried to stop him and get justice for Garcia, none of their attacks reached their intended target, and Carmine smiled at one of his attackers, just one. That one attacker then turned and killed the other twelve attackers, before killing himself. On seeing this, all thoughts of attack vanished, and the mages followed suit. This is a direct quote from Henry Carmine on that day. 'The All-Powers are here to rule. Now we finally do.' Carmine continued to rule as Prime Mage for seventy years through fear and intimidation, using regular public executions to remind people not to attempt to cross him. In the year 467 he was ousted by a revolution of three hundred mages storming the Imperium houses, Henry Carmine used mind control and his own powers to kill one hundred and eighty of those storming the building, but he ran when he realised that even he was outnumbered. The revolution was led by a mage by the name of Agnese Salvatar, who was then elected as Prime Mage where she remained for the next thirty four years. In the year 501 a final attack against Carmine was staged with Prime Mage Salvatar leading it. Every single mage involved in the attack, which numbered three hundred and fifty mages and Carmine, a total of three hundred and fifty one mages died when Carmine knew it was his last fight and used a build-up of fire magic to explode himself. Killing himself and taking as many mages with him as he could. Henry Carmine died aged 127." Professor Horton continued to detail other major events in Henry Carmines life until the lesson was over, and he dismissed the class.

As the rest of the class was leaving, Aaron stepped towards Professor Horton. "Professor, I have a few questions, but not about the lesson. If that's ok."

The professor looked up and smiled. "I thought you might Mr Scott, please go ahead."

"Well, one's about ages." Aaron began but the professor interrupted.

"Ah, is it why did they live so long?" He asked.

Aaron tilted his head, he had not actually thought of that. "Well yeah, now that you mention it. But the one I was going to ask is how age worked out, on Nerium? Alexander Miller died aged 102, but was only on Nerium for eighty six years. To me that says that his sixteen years on Earth was taken into account, am I right?" The professor nodded. "So how old are we, are we 42 or are we 16?"

"Another interesting question, one that not many people ask." Professor Horton smiled. "I do like rare questions. You are correct, the years on earth are taken into account. So that makes you all forty two years old, though, over time most mages revert to something close to their teenage selves." He smiled while shuffling through papers on his desk. "Now, onto the longevity of mages, there are theories as to why we live so long here. There is the fact that the years are shorter here and some believe that because we have and use magic that that extends our lives, some suggest it could be something else about Nerium itself. But most mages live well into their one hundreds." He smiled at Aaron again. "Did you say you had another question?"

Aaron nodded as he took in the professor's answer. "Yes, it's a bit more personal. I've been told that there is one professor here that was on Nerium when Alexander Miller was alive." The professor smiled. "Is that you?"

“It is me.” He admitted. “Although I was only halfway through my first year when he was killed, I do remember the fear floating through the air. Not knowing where he would attack next, and the relief when he was finally defeated.” He looked at Aaron with a thoughtful look on his face. “I must say, Mr Scott. I have been expecting you to disagree with my lessons. Files have shown that all All-Powers do, I have also been informed that you have a book with a different version of history.”

“I have.” Aaron admitted. “I’ve been told that All-Powers disagree with your lessons too. That’s why I’ve chosen not to read my book until after your lessons. I’m hoping that I can come into the History of Nerium classes, with no idea of what’s coming. Then I’ll read the same chapter in my book and hopefully find parts where they overlap, surely there has to be some truth to both versions.” Aaron looked down. “I don’t want to believe that every single All-Power has gone bad. Thank you, professor.”

11

"Well then boys and girls, are you sitting comfortably?" Aaron, Tala, Ajit, and Amelie were in Aarons room. Aaron had *An accurate history of The All-Power* open on his lap. "Then let's have the same lesson from a different perspective."

He was trying to make jokes about it for his own benefit more than for anyone else, he really was not looking forward to reading about Henry Carmine from the books twisted view of All-Powers.

Tala must have noticed his hesitation. "You know one of us would read it if we could." She said smiling at him.

He smiled back at her. "I know." Then he looked back down to the book. "OK then, here we go.

Henry Carmine 390-501

Henry Carmine faced multiple attacks during his time at Doctrina from his professors and the lesser mage students, he left every attack uninjured but left every attacking lesser mage with just enough life left in their bodies to send a message to any lesser mage foolish enough to attack him in the future.

Henry Carmine knew from the very beginning that he could be incredible and so he honed his skills to perfection.

After graduating, Henry Carmine sought employment in the Imperium houses knowing it would only be a matter of time before he would take his rightful place as the Prime Mage to rule.

He was assigned a menial position, which he accepted, knowing he would be quickly promoted. The Prime Mage of the time, Prime Mage Garcia had other ideas, he went out of his way to ensure that Henry Carmine never moved up from that menial position. He went as far as to hold regular private meetings to belittle and antagonise Henry Carmine.

After three years of taking this torture Henry Carmine finally accepted his role on this world, during one of the torturous meetings, Henry Carmine removed the Prime Mages head with a swipe of his finger. Henry Carmine then walked proudly through the halls of the Imperium houses displaying his victory, he knew he would have to display his power to subdue his new staff. The attack that came was expected, but once again Henry Carmine remained uninjured. Using the skills he had perfected he chose one of his attackers, an Air mage, and mentally instructed him to destroy the other foolish lesser mages.

Once the lesser mage had completed this task, he expanded an air bubble within his own head and sent a final message to the rest of Prime Mage Carmines new staff.

Cementing his new position Henry Carmine declared. 'The All-Powers are here to rule. Now we finally do.'

Henry Carmine remained in his rightful position for the next seventy years by continually thinning the heard of lesser mages, until a lesser mage named Agnese Salvatar raised an army of lesser mages large enough to overwhelm Henry Carmine in an unlawful coup.

For thirty four years Henry Carmine fought to regain his rightful position, and for thirty four years the traitorous Salvatar raised an even larger army, and in the year 501 the lesser mage army stormed Henry Carmines home.

Henry Carmine refused to allow the lesser mages to decide his death, he fought his way to their very centre and used Fire and Air magic to turn his own body into a bomb, killing every mage there, including himself.

Henry Carmine should be remembered as a hero to all All-Powers, he died in the year 501 aged just 127.

That's everything it says for Carmine." Aaron finished and looked up at the rest of the group.

"OK, well there isn't anything all that different from what Professor Horton told us, just from the books distorted view of it." Ajit was the first to speak, he looked to the two girls. "Unless I'm missing something."

Amelie looked thoughtful for a moment. "No, I don't think you are." She said, shaking her head. "The events are the same but there is something that's bugging me. The quote 'The All-Powers are here to rule, now we finally do.' There's something about that, but I can't place it."

"It's from the last page of the book." Tala answered her, when everyone else looked at her she added. "After it said that Isabella Lockton created the book."

Aaron flicked to the last page to check. "You're right, it says it here. *We the All-Powers are here to rule.*" He looked up at Tala. "How did you remember that?" She just shrugged and Aaron looked down at the page while the other three chatted.

Aaron was still thinking about Henry Carmine when he went to sleep that night, he could not understand what could have happened in someone's life to make them like that.

*

Aaron was gliding down a corridor he did not recognise, there were two people gliding behind him, he could feel their vibrations on the air.

He was angry.

One of his closest advisors had been working against him for years, he could feel the stab of pain from the disloyalty within him. He could also feel the sense of impending justice as he glided down the long corridor. He was eager to put a permanent end to the treachery.

He reached the end of the corridor and entered a large hall with three throne like chairs set on a stage, and a man chained in a pit in the middle of the room.

Aaron felt his anger grow into a rage that filled him as he looked at the man, but the rage seemed to calm him. He floated to the centre chair and sat down as the two others sat either side of him, Aaron did not look at them.

Instead, he stared intently at the man chained in the centre of the room, it was then that he noticed it was not a man, it was a teenage boy. It was Ajit, he had been beaten, his left eye was swollen and there was dried blood down the same side of his head.

"Ajit Shah, what do you have to say for yourself?" Tala's voice came from Aarons right.

Aaron did not turn to look at her, his gaze never left Ajit. His rage turning into a fury that burned within him, impatient, yearning to be set free. Longing to carry out the sentence this deceitful rat justly deserved.

Ajit looked at the three of them with nothing but contempt. "You're all monsters, why would you do any of this?" He spat at them, straining against his chains.

"We, are not the monsters here. You, are the one that betrayed us." Amelie's venom filled voice came from Aarons left, Aaron's glare still did not leave Ajit.

"Because I didn't agree that anyone who disagreed with us should be killed? That isn't a betrayal Amelie, that is just human decency!" Ajit shouted back at her. "Why can't you see that what you're doing is wrong?" He stopped talking when Aaron raised a hand.

Aaron looked at his hand, moving his gaze from Ajit for the first time since he had entered the room. His palm was facing up, above his palm he felt the air and hardened it into the shape of a long spike. His breath was shaking with excitement, as he felt the moment he had been waiting for draw closer. He slowly moved the spike toward Ajit's head, watching as it moved.

Ajit noticed this and started begging. "Aaron, no!" He shouted as he tried to move backwards, away from Aaron. "Aaron, you don't want to do this, you've never wanted this, you fought against this for so long." He reached the full extent of his bonds, but he kept pulling. The shackles on his wrists cutting into him and drawing even more blood. "Aaron please don't do this!" He felt the spike tip gently press against and slowly dig into the centre of his forehead, drawing fresh blood that slowly ran down the centre of his face and mixed with the dried blood under his nose. "Aaron please, we were friends." He pleaded with his captor.

Tala's voice rang throughout the room drowning out Ajit's pleas. "There is only one suitable outcome for a betrayal like yours."

Aaron changed the shape of the spike, changing it to form a band, wrapping around Ajit's head. Aaron tightened it slowly so that Ajit could feel the pressure, so he would know what was coming. Ajit began to scream.

"Ajit Shah, your betrayal warrants only one thing. Death." Tala's voice boomed, drowning out Ajit's screams, finally voicing the sentence Aaron had been longing to hear.

Aaron continued tightening the band, blood began to leak out of Ajit's nose, mixing with the fresh and dried blood that was already there. Ajit continued to scream, Aaron continued to tighten the band, Ajit's skull began to crack, tighter and tighter, Ajit's head exploded.

Ajit's body fell to the ground, the left side of his head missing, his lifeless right eye staring up at Aaron.

*

Aaron woke with a scream of his own, drenched in sweat and tangled in his bed sheets.

12

Aaron could not bring himself to look at Ajit for the next few days and could barely concentrate on his lessons. Healing was a theory lesson and all his dual mage lessons continued with ways to safely deflect attacks, in his self-study sessions he searched through his books trying to find anything he could about dreams, but he found nothing.

He had just finished eating his lunch on Friday when Tala leaned in and whispered to him. “Let’s go for a walk.” He nodded and the two got up and left the main hall. “OK, spit it out. What’s bothering you?” She said when they were close to the lone tree, which had become the groups go to spot for quiet conversations.

Aaron looked at her for a moment, thinking about lying to her. But the determination in her eyes told him she knew there was something wrong and that she was not going to just let it go. “I had a dream.” He confessed, and he told her every detail of the dream, feeling both worried and relieved as he did. “I haven’t even been able to look at Ajit since.”

Tala said nothing as he explained and just nodded as he finished. “Were we old?” She finally asked.

“Well, I didn’t look at you or Amelie, but Ajit looked exactly like he does now.”

She nodded again. “Did you recognise the room we were all in?” He shook his head. “To be honest, I think it’s just because you were worried about what we read in your book. Like, you read that and you’re already worried and then you went to sleep, and your worries and that chapter combined to give you a bad dream. Maybe that’s all it was, a bad dream.”

“Maybe.” Aaron said quietly, but he was not convinced. “But it seemed so real, I can’t get the image of Ajit’s body lying in front of me with half of his head missing out of my mind.” Aaron shuddered and shook his head. “And now we have another history lesson.” He sighed.

She smiled at him and grabbed hold of his hand. “Just try and put it out of your mind.” She said as they walked hand in hand to the lesson Aaron was starting to hate. They saw Amelie and Ajit waiting outside Professor Hortons office, the two of them noticed Aaron and Tala walking hand in hand and raised their eyebrows, Ajit with a questioning look and Amelie with a smile on her face. “Now they won’t ask what we’ve been talking about.” Tala whispered to Aaron as she whipped her hand away.

Aaron smirked at her and sarcastically whispered back. “Yeah, because that’s the only reason.” She blushed and he immediately felt better for talking to her.

They got to the office and before Amelie or Ajit could say anything, Professor Horton opened the door and ushered them all inside. “Good afternoon everyone.” He said as they all sat down. “Todays session is a little different, Mr Scott, could you please give us the names of the next two All-Powers.” He asked as he walked to his desk and leaned against it.

Aaron had been expecting this and had already memorised the names of every All-Power from the contents page of his book. “Next there is Anastasia Solovyov and before her was Aban Fasil.”

The professor nodded. “Absolutely correct. So far you have learnt about Alexander Miller, who disappeared for over fifty years and then went on a worldwide killing spree, and Henry Carmine, who installed himself as the Prime Mage and ruled Nerium through fear and public executions.” He began as he moved around his desk and sat behind it. “Like I said this is a little different, we will begin with Aban Fasil, he arrived on Nerium in the year 253. At this point there had not been an All-Power for seventy three years and the magical community at the time was, without giving too much of the next lesson away, a little ashamed of themselves. Unlike both Miller and Carmine, Fasil was not attacked by either students or professors, and he excelled while here at Doctrina. He is the first of just two All-Powers not to choose to remain at Doctrina for four years, instead opting to leave after his third year. He started a farm and fed his local village for the next four years, he was reportedly very friendly and very popular.”

He looked to Aaron with the smallest of smiles. “In the year 260 Fasil returned to Doctrina when Anastasia Solovyov arrived, as the only All-Power alive he was the only choice for professor to teach a newly discovered All-Power. Like Fasil, Solovyov did not face attacks and she also excelled for her three years here. She, being the second All-Power to opt to leave school after her third year. The two All-Powers returned together to Fasil’s farm and over the years became pillars of their little community, they lived on the farm happily and event free together, for one hundred and fifteen years.”

Aaron felt hope blossom within him. A hundred and fifteen years with nothing bad happening, perhaps these were the All-Powers he had been hoping to hear about.

“During this time however.” Professor Horton continued. “On the farthest side of human populated Nerium, an unexplainable and uncurable plague relentlessly worked its way across the planet. Mages would be found dead, covered with boils and with hair missing, they would be fine and happy one day and dead the next. It began with one person a month and then two, then a family, then a village and so on. Thousands died from this plague, until the year 378 when the plagues source was discovered. A traveller heading toward a village to gain lodging for the night heard tortured screams mixed with high pitched laughter. The traveller hid until the screaming stopped and he glimpsed a man and a woman walk out into the open, share a kiss and then vanish into a green light.”

Aaron slumped in his chair, the hope that had been swelling inside him bursting like a popped balloon.

“The traveller reported this to the closest authorities.” The professor went on. “Those authorities relayed the information to the Prime Mage, who travelled to the farm of Fasil and Solovyov. A total of one hundred mages carefully and quietly surrounded the farm as the Prime Mage, Prime Mage Horton, no relation as far as I know.” He added with a smile. “Approached the Farmhouse. Fasil and Solovyov kindly greeted the Prime Mage, until the Prime questioned them about the plague. Solovyov simply tilted her head and the Prime fell screaming to the ground with boils erupting all over him, as the Prime lay dying the one hundred mages leapt from their hiding places and attacked the All-Powers.

With a quick glance at Aaron, the professor continued. “Fasil defended as Solovyov clicked her fingers and mages around her erupted into flames. After seventy eight of those mages had died, one of the remaining mages, it is unknown which one, managed to injure Solovyov. Fasil let out a horrified scream and leapt to her aid, and the two vanished into a green light. Never to be seen or heard from again. It is assumed that Solovyov died from her injuries and, heartbroken, Fasil remained in isolation until his own death. The last time either was ever seen was the year 378.” He looked around the group and his eyes settled on Aaron. “Any questions?”

Aaron nodded. “You said that Anastasia killed the Prime Mage with the plague and that Aban defended, is there any evidence that he ever killed anyone?” He asked, as the burst balloon of hope within him started to slightly inflate once more.

“I thought you would pick up on that, no.” The professor smiled and nodded. “No, Mr Scott. There is no evidence that Fasil ever actually killed anyone. What we can deduct from what the history books tell us, is that Fasil and Solovyov were in love and that Fasil would have done anything that Solovyov wanted and anything to protect her.” Again, he smiled at Aaron. “Fasil could be one of the only All-Powers to have not wanted a war, he was complicit, but it seems that it may never have been his aim.”

“I have another question, professor. You’re teaching these as wars, but a war is when two nations fight each other.” Aaron began. “I’m not disagreeing with the events.” He added, not wanting to sound like every other All-Power that the professor had heard about. “But aren’t these just serial killers and mass murderers? By claiming that they are wars, are you not giving these killers more credit than they deserve?”

“Interesting.” The professor said quietly and thoughtfully. “On Earth yes, a war is when two nations fight. But on Nerium that has never happened, that is also a question that has never been asked. And to be frank, a question that I, myself have never considered. It has always been taught that these were wars. I shall give that some thought and get back to you.”

Head Mistress Taylor was waiting in the corridor for Aaron when the History of Nerium lesson ended, as the dual mages went on to their dual lessons, Aaron followed the head mistress to her office for their first weekly interview. “Please, take a seat Mr Scott.” She said, gesturing to the chair in front of the desk once they had entered her office.

The head mistress’s office was a large room in a corner of the school on the top floor, its black walls covered with paintings and bookcases. There was a fireplace with three armchairs around it. It also had two windows with views of the rolling hills of the school grounds and Nerium beyond.

“I’m hearing good things from your professors, how has your first week been for you?” She asked Aaron as he sat down.

“It’s been, interesting.” Aaron let out a sigh. “I’m not quite sure I believed all the All-Power hype, until all the professors pointed out how fast I was picking things up compared to other mages.”

She nodded at him. “Yes, in just a few days you mastered shields that take even the most talented mages weeks to learn and others months. Anything else? How about the History of Nerium sessions?”

"I decided not to read my book ahead of the lessons, so I've only been reading what Professor Horton has already taught us. There aren't massive differences to be honest. Just a difference in perspective, the book has most of the same events just saying that the All-Powers were right to do what they were doing." Aaron left out the fact that he had shared the books versions with his friends.

"Why not read them before?" She asked him.

"Well." Aaron began thoughtfully. "When I first read the book, I read Alexander Millers chapter, and to be honest, it scared me. Then you said that every All-Power disagreed with the history lessons." He looked out of the window. "I don't want to be like every other All-Power, especially the turning bad and killing people part." He continued, looking back to the head mistress. "I didn't want to read the book after that first time, every chapter I've read so far still feels like propaganda, like it's trying to convince All-Powers that they are better than everyone else. It repeatedly refers to other mages as 'lesser mages' and says things about ruling." He stopped for a moment to look out of the office window again. "The last lesson though, that's given me a little hope. Hearing how Aban Fasil was a farmer and liked by the people he lived near and how he might not have killed anyone, but how he might have acted out of love." Once again, he looked back to the head mistress. "If Anastasia had never arrived as an All-Power, he could have lived a quiet and normal life."

She nodded again. “It is a possibility, one that we can never know for sure I’m afraid.” She observed him for a moment. “What about your friends, I take it they are still your friends.”

Aaron thought of Tala and smiled. “They are.”

“Glad to hear that.” She smiled then let out a sigh. “As I have not heard anything about any attacks, shall I assume there have been none?” Aaron nodded. “These interviews are procedure, Mr Scott. But I see no reason to pry any deeper into your life at this point. I will pass what I and the other professors have observed to the Prime Mage, and I will see you again in here next Friday.”

Aaron walked through the school enjoying how quiet it was while everyone else was still in their lessons, he followed his feet without worry, the dream all but forgotten as Aban Fasil had given him a tiny flicker of hope. He noticed he was heading towards the lone tree and smiled, the book could wait till Sunday, he was going to hold on to that tiny glimmer of hope for the next few days.

13

The weekend passed with Aaron, Tala, Amelie, and Ajit laughing and joking, the four of them practicing air shields and Aaron showing the other three the Earth, Air and Ice shields he had learnt. He was unable to show them how he was doing with diverting attacks, as none of them knew how to attack yet.

Sunday evening came around very quickly and the four of them were once again in Aarons room to read *An accurate history of The All-Power*'s version of Aban Fasil and Anastasia Solovyov.

Aaron picked the book from the shelf and turned to sit in the armchair, only to find Amelie sat in it smiling at him, he turned to see a space next to Tala on the sofa.

“Subtle.” He said to Amelie with a chuckle, she just shrugged, and he sat down next to Tala. He leafed through the pages until he got to the beginning of Aban Fasil’s chapter. “OK, here we go. There isn’t much for Aban,

Aban Fasil 253-394

Aban Fasil’s time at Doctrina was uneventful.

Aban Fasil chose a life of servitude for lesser mages, tending a farm to feed them.

Aban Fasil was nothing until the arrival of Anastasia Solovyov.

Aban Fasil died shamefully in the year 394 aged 157.

Wow. That's his entire chapter, the book really doesn't like him." Aaron finished with his eyebrows raised. He looked up at the other three, a little disheartened by the books view of Aban, but they didn't look concerned by what he had just read to them, he looked back to the book and continued reading aloud.

"Anastasia Solovyov 260-378

Anastasia Solovyov emerged as an All-Power just seven years after the emergence of Aban Fasil. Aban Fasil returned to Doctrina as the only All-Power professor in the history of Nerium. Aban Fasil taught Anastasia Solovyov everything he knew and the two learnt more together. Anastasia Solovyov learnt how to turn healing magic into a weapon, Aban Fasil learnt how to open a doorway to other parts of Nerium.

Anastasia Solovyov left Doctrina after three years of Aban Fasil's tutelage and joined Aban Fasil at his shameful farm. Anastasia Solovyov and Aban Fasil fell in love and Anastasia Solovyov confessed her desire to destroy the lesser mages. Aban Fasil had become very skilled at denying his true self and for a time convinced Anastasia Solovyov to ignore her true self also. Although the two continued to talk about Anastasia Solovyov's calling. Eventually, Anastasia Solovyov convinced Aban Fasil to let her destroy just one lesser mage, Aban Fasil opened a door to another part of Nerium and together the pair found a lesser mage living alone and Anastasia Solovyov used her healing magic to kill the lesser mage.

Aban Fasil saw how happy this made Anastasia Solovyov and so he allowed her to destroy more lesser mages each month in that same area of Nerium. The pairs love for each other grew along with Anastasia Solovyov's desire to destroy the lesser mages.

Aban Fasil took Anastasia Solovyov from village to village on the other side of Nerium to where the pair lived in order to allow her to continue with her mission. For over a century Anastasia Solovyov silently decimated the lesser mages until one night, Anastasia Solovyov was certain she had just destroyed an entire settlement of the lesser mages and she happily returned to the home her, and Aban Fasil had made for themselves.

What Anastasia Solovyov did not know was that a lesser mage had been sneaking in the shadows like the rat he was, this rat saw Anastasia Solovyov and Aban Fasil leave the settlement and reported to the Prime Mage of the time, Prime Mage Horton.

Prime Mage Horton needed no more reason to attack the All-Powers at their home, he and one hundred other lesser mages surrounded the home of Anastasia Solovyov and Aban Fasil.

Aban Fasil, the failure of an All-Power, wanted to negotiate with the Prime Mage and so the two spoke for a while, until Anastasia Solovyov grew tired of the Prime Mage's presence. With a tilt of her head Anastasia Solovyov killed the Prime Mage with her healing magic and the remaining lesser mages attacked.
Aban Fasil protected Anastasia Solovyov from the attacks, perhaps his only redeeming act, enabling Anastasia Solovyov to snap her fingers and cause lesser mages to erupt in flames. The All-Powers had nearly killed every attacking lesser mage when one of the attacks hit Anastasia Solovyov killing her instantly. Aban Fasil screamed in horror and took her body to a cave in the mountains where he remained until his own death.

Anastasia Solovyov killed more lesser mages than any other All-Power. Anastasia Solovyov died a hero in the year 378 aged 134."

He finished reading and looked up at the others wondering what they thought of that version.

For a moment no one said anything. “You were right Aaron.” Amelie said, breaking the silence. “Fasil didn’t hurt anyone, it was definitely his idea to kill mages on the other side of Nerium. But he didn’t kill anyone himself.”

“Why do you think it was his idea?” Ajit asked.

“Do you think Solovyov would have cared about killing people in her own village? Or that Fasil took her to the other side of the planet so that no one would suspect that it was them killing mages?” None of them needed to answer, when she put it like that, it was obvious to everyone.

Aaron reread the chapter once everyone had left, happy that he had found Aban Fasil, an All-Power that would have had a normal life if he had not met Anastasia Solovyov. But at the same time, he could not help but be disappointed at how the book portrayed him, was that how the book would tell Aaron’s story in the future?

*

Aaron was in the Water Fire dual classroom with a girl who he did not recognise. “Professor Scott.” The girl said nervously. “I don’t think I’m going to stay here for a fourth year.”

Aaron looked at her and smiled. “That is, of course, your choice to make, Miss Shackleton. As an All-Power you can choose whether or not you continue here at Doctrina for a fourth year.”

Miss Shackleton looked down at her feet. “Perhaps, I could come and live with you.” She looked up at him. “That way we can come up with a plan.”

Aaron was confused. “I’m not sure I understand you, Miss Shackleton. A plan for what?”

“We can work together, together we could be incredible. That’s where Aban Fasil and Anastasia Solovyov went wrong, they didn’t work together. If Aban hadn’t been so weak, they could have got rid of all those lesser mages, and then trained all the new lesser mages that arrived each year to worship them.” She looked excited now. “That’s what we could do. We, we could surprise them and take out Prime Mage Ramos first and then kill anyone who gets in our way.”

“Miss Shackleton, Caitlin. I know why you are feeling this way. But we don’t need to do any of that.” Aaron said understandingly. “I remember having thoughts like that when I was a student here. But you can choose not to live like that, we are no better than anyone else just because we are All-Powers.”

Caitlin looked a little confused for a moment. “Professor, do you remember *An accurate history of The All-Power*?” She asked.

“Of course I do, I still have my copy.” He answered, smiling at her.

“Do you know what it says about you?” Caitlin continued to question him.

He shook his head. “I have not looked at my chapter in almost three decades.”

She looked at him with tears in her eyes. “Unless he changes his ways, Aaron Scott is destined to die as the biggest disgrace to the name All-Power.” The tears now flowing down her cheeks. “Please professor, please let me help you become what you always should have been.”

Aaron smiled softly at her. “Miss Shackleton, just concentrate on your remaining few months here. You have your interview with Head Mistress Durand. Go to that, and I will see you in here on Monday.” She nodded, wiped her face, and left.

Aaron waited a few seconds, opened a green doorway, and stepped through into his office, he walked straight to his bookshelf. He picked up *An accurate history of The All-Power* and threw the pages over until he reached his own chapter,

Aaron Scott 763 –

Aaron Scott showed great potential upon his arrival at Doctrina surviving multiple attacks. Aaron Scott was extremely powerful, learning quickly and even teaching two dual mages things that no other dual mage had ever achieved.

Aaron Scott left Doctrina after four years and worked in a menial position in the Imperium houses. Aaron Scott could have destroyed Prime Mage Reid and claimed his rightful place at any time. He did not.

Aaron Scott watched as years went by and a new Prime Mage was elected, one of the lesser dual mages he had known while at Doctrina. Again, Aaron Scott could have destroyed this new Prime at any time. Again, he did not.

Aaron Scott returned to Doctrina in the year 795 on the emergence of a new All-Power, Caitlin Shackleton.

Aaron Scott taught as the All-Power professor well but, unless he changes his ways, Aaron Scott is destined to die as the biggest disgrace to the name All-Power there has ever been.

Aaron stood in his office reading and rereading the page over and over until it was seared into his mind, and it became unfocused.

*

Aaron woke in his bed, now with a new dream to be troubled by.

14

“I had a weird dream last night.” Aaron said as he sat down for breakfast the next day and he proceeded to tell Tala, Ajit, and Amelie all about it. He and Tala had already decided not to tell the other two about his first dream, she looked a little shocked that he had shared this one.

"It’s just a dream, probably because how bad the book treated Fasil.” Amelie said sounding unconcerned.

Tala smiled. “At least I get to be the Prime Mage.”

“Wait a minute.” Ajit said, in between shovelling handfuls of gruel into his mouth. “Where was I? Amelie is the Head of this place and Tala is the Prime Mage, what am I doing?” He laughed.

Aaron just shrugged and didn’t say anything, he was glad that Ajit wasn’t in this new dream considering what had happened to him in Aaron’s last dream.

“I’m sure you were doing something important.” Amelie said as she laid her hand on Ajit’s, Aaron and Tala noticed this and shared a knowing look.

“Are we getting new timetables today?” Aaron asked. The other three looked at him, all of them looking puzzled. “What?” He asked them.

"Why would we get new timetables? The ones we got last week were for the whole year." Ajit said.

Amelie nodded. "Yeah, they had last weeks lessons and then a new week which covered the rest of the year."

Puzzled, Aaron pulled out his timetable to check. It had 'Week one' written on the top, he showed the others. As they were all discussing why he didn't have a timetable for the whole year, a rolled-up piece of paper was thrust in front of Aaron's face. Aaron looked up to see the head mistress smile at him as she took his old timetable back.

"You only had a timetable for last week." Head Mistress Taylor said, as though she knew exactly what the four of them had been speaking about. "Because, the professors and I, were unsure how you would be able to manage switching between disciplines. I think you will find your new timetable more stable." She smiled and walked away.

Aaron unrolled the paper on the table as the group all looked at it.

Monday

1. History of Nerium - Professor Hortons office
2. Air Fire dual – Air Fire Classroom one
3. Lunch
4. Air Fire dual – Air Fire Classroom one
5. All-Power self-study

Tuesday

1. Earth Water dual – Earth Water Classroom one
2. Lunch
3. Earth Air dual – Earth Air Classroom one

4. All-Power self-study

Wednesday

1. Earth Air dual – Earth Air Classroom
2. Water Fire dual – Water Fire Classroom
3. Lunch
4. Water Fire dual – Water Fire Classroom
5. All-Power self-study

Thursday

1. Healing – Healing classroom one
2. Air Fire dual – Air Fire Classroom one
3. Lunch
4. Earth Water dual – Earth Water Classroom one
5. Earth Air dual – Earth Air Classroom

Friday

1. Water Fire dual – Water Fire Classroom
2. All-Power self-study
3. Lunch
4. History of Nerium – Professor Hortons office
5. Meeting with Head Mistress Taylor, Head Mistress' office.

Tala let out an excited squeal and gripped Aaron's arm. "You're with us almost all day." She said beaming up at him.

Aaron couldn't help but smile at her excitement and as the group stood, he took her hand in his and held it as they walked to their first class.

“Good morning, everyone.” Professor Horton smiled as Aaron and the dual mages sat down. “I trust you are all well rested from the weekend. Mr Scott, if you wouldn’t mind, the names of the last two All-Powers.”

Aaron nodded. “Nicholas Garnier and the first All-Power was Isabella Lockton.”

“Excellent.” Professor Horton smiled and continued. “These are the last two All-Powers. And, in a moment you will understand why we are covering both in one session. Nicholas Garnier.” The professor let out a strained breath. “Nicholas Garnier arrived at Doctrina in the year 178 and on his emergence as an All-Power the staff at Doctrina refused to teach him, instead they chained him up in the main hall. For two years. I will let that sink in, they chained Garnier up in the main hall for two years.” He looked around the group.

Aaron couldn’t be sure how the rest of the group felt about this because his gaze did not leave the professor, but he felt disgusted. What right did they have to do that to an All-Power?

The professor let out a sigh and continued. “Just one professor felt pity for Garnier, and she fed him daily, she explained why the other professors had decided to keep him chained and why they refused to teach him. Over the two years that he was chained up he taught himself to meditate and through this, he somehow taught himself magic, eventually he was able to break free of his chains and crawl out of the main hall, however he only made it to the courtyard before he was found and beaten to death by three professors.” He looked around the room again.

This time, Aaron looked around as well. Tala and Amelie looked disgusted by what they had just heard. Ajit, Tobias, and Isla looked mildly interested but they weren't showing the disgust that Tala and Amelie were. Aaron was struggling to hide the anger that was building inside him, he felt as though his blood was beginning to boil within his veins. How dare they? How dare they do that to an All-Power?

The professor continued. "On to Isabella Lockton. Lockton arrived on Nerium with the first humans, making her arrival in the year 0. When the first one hundred humans got here, they somehow already knew that they had abilities, and they knew what they could and couldn't do. Lockton took the lead and by the time the next one hundred humans arrived a year later, she had established order in the panic. She quickly discovered that the newest arrivals did not already know about their abilities, nor did they know how to use them, by the time the third lot of new arrivals appeared on Nerium, Isabella Lockton had built Doctrina single handed. Isabella Lockton used her All-Power abilities to build this very school."

Amelie and Tala looked at Aaron, he did not look back, instead he stayed focused on Professor Horton.

“As the years went by and no new All-Powers arrived with the yearly arrivals, Lockton began to believe she was special. Lockton held on to her position as the leader of the community, it was her that named the position as the Prime Mage, choosing the word prime as it meant ‘of first importance’ or ‘of the best quality’. More and more years passed and no new All-Powers arrived. In the year 75 Lockton declared herself the God of all mages, as she alone could perform every branch of magic and even other magics that no other mage could. Two other mages tried to convince her that she had been in the position of Prime Mage too long and the responsibilities were getting on top of her, they tried to get her to step down, to allow an election to find someone to replace her. They did this publicly, so to prove to others that she was indeed the God of all mages, she held out a hand and pulled every drop of moisture from the two mages, killing them with ease in front of every mage present. For the next one hundred and one year’s, Lockton remained in the position of Prime Mage, killing anyone brave enough to stand up to her, fear grew and spread within the other mages and in the year 176 they banded together to confront her. Lockton did not go quietly, she killed almost two hundred more mages before she was overpowered. Her last words were. ‘There will be an All-Power that will rule Nerium for eternity, they will teach this world the meaning of fear.’ And then she faded from existence, at the time, it was presumed that that was how All-Powers died. She has never been seen since, so it is the common decision that she chose to end her life rather than give up power. Over the one hundred and seventy six years of her rule on Nerium Isabella Lockton killed nearly one thousand mages. She died in the year 176 aged 192. Any questions?”

Aaron barely heard any questions or the rest of the lesson.

"I guess we know why your room is so much better than ours now." Amelie said as the four of them walked up the stairs to Air Fire Classroom one. "This school was built by the first All-Power. It's obvious that she wasn't afraid of All-Powers."

Aaron nodded, still a little angry at how Nicholas Garnier had been treated. "Yeah, that's one less question."

Professor Flak walked to Aaron after she had observed the progress the dual mages had made. "You have been helping Miss Durand and Miss Ramos practice haven't you." She said with a smile.

Aaron nodded. "And Ajit, Mr Shah. I've been helping all of them."

"I can tell, he has made a lot of progress. Not as much as Miss Durand and Miss Ramos though, in fact they'll be joining you with deflection spells, thanks to your help."

She motioned to Tala and Amelie and the two girls came over to join them. Aaron smiled happily at the two of them but inside he felt a stab of worry creep in, from his dream the night before. Something from his page in the dream. Something about dual mages.

Aaron Scott was extremely powerful, learning quickly and even teaching two dual mages things that no other dual mage had ever achieved.

But it was just a dream, wasn't it?

Aaron sat in his library during his self-study session later that day, still thinking about his dream and Tala and Amelie's progress from shields to deflection. Why wasn't Ajit in this new dream? He still couldn't find anything about dreams on his bookshelves. He had to find out if these were just dreams or if they were something more. But he had no idea how he could do that.

He was still contemplating this when his friends knocked on his door an hour later, he let them in and followed them back into his library. He noticed Ajit looked a little down. "Ajit, are you alright?"

"Yeah, just a little pissed off that I didn't get moved to deflection as well." He shrugged. "Don't worry about it."

Amelie smiled and linked her arm through his as she sat next to him on the sofa. "You will, we'll get more practice in."

Aaron agreed. "Yeah absolutely, we can practice every second we can. We'll all work together. You three are going to be the best dual mages in this planet's history."

Ajit looked a little happier. "Alright fine, I'll actually practice then. Let's get back to your book."

"OK then, let's do this one last time." Aaron said as he picked up *An accurate history of The All-Power*. "You all ready?" They all nodded as he sat in the armchair. "Here we go,

Nicholas Garnier 178-180

Nicholas Garnier arrived on Nerium just two years after Isabella Lockton's vanishing.

When Nicholas Garnier emerged as an All-Power the professors at Doctrina refused to teach him, instead they chained him up in the main hall of Doctrina school and left him there with no explanation. Nicholas Garnier was left chained and humiliated in full view of the entire school.

One professor did not agree however, the healing professor fed Nicholas Garnier and explained to him why the other professors had done what they had done.

Before arriving on Nerium Nicholas Garnier's family had been a spiritual family, he used meditation techniques he had learnt as a child to meditate during his many hours of solitude. Through meditation he was able to speak with Isabella Lockton, she was able to teach him how to break from his restraints. It took a year and a half, but Nicholas Garnier was eventually able to break his bonds, however, his legs lacked the strength to carry him from Doctrina. Nicholas Garnier attempted to crawl away from his captors but was beaten and kicked to death by the professors of Doctrina.

Nicholas Garnier was murdered before he could discover who he was. Nicholas Garnier died in the year 180 aged just 18."

Tala, Amelie, and Ajit all erupted into questions.

"He actually taught himself magic?" Tala asked.

"How did meditation help him?" Ajit questioned.

"He spoke to Lockton?" Amelie added.

Aaron did not answer any of them, his eyes never left the page in front of him, he was fighting a sudden burst of anger, his blood was boiling in his veins once more. How dare they? How dare they chain up an All-Power? Garnier should have learnt how to destroy them all from Lockton. Aaron shook his head trying to shake those thoughts from his mind.

He threw the pages back to the beginning of Isabella Lockton's chapter. "Quiet, let's find out about Isabella,

Isabella Lockton 0"

"Hold on, she doesn't have a death date!" Amelie interrupted him.

"Shhh!" Tala silenced her.

Aaron continued.

"Isabella Lockton was one of the first humans to arrive on Nerium, while others were confused and afraid, Isabella Lockton knew her powers were limitless.

Over the next year Isabella Lockton created order and community, when new mages arrived on Nerium she was not surprised. Isabella Lockton quickly ascertained that these new mages did not know of their powers, and she established Doctrina school and placed professors to teach the new mages. When the third year came round, and more new mages arrived Isabella Lockton had built the school in its entirety."

"Wait! Why isn't the book calling everyone lesser mages, like it normally does?" Ajit interrupted.

Aaron ignored him and carried on.

"Over the next decade Isabella Lockton established government and built the Imperium houses, she set up the post of Prime Mage and, as she had led the mages since the beginning of humans populating Nerium, she filled the post herself.

Another decade passed and Prime Mage Lockton noticed that not one new All-Power had arrived. After two more decades passed and still no other All-Powers had emerged, Prime Mage Lockton began to delve deeper into her own abilities.

For the next thirty five years, Prime Mage Lockton led Nerium as the mage community began to spread around their new world. All the while she delved into her powers.

After thirty five years of searching her own abilities, Prime Mage Lockton knew that there was not a single mage on the planet of Nerium that could match her. Prime Mage Lockton was a god among ants.

Prime Mage Lockton informed the other mages that were so much less than she was, of her discovery, and they mocked her. Two of the lessers attempted to persuade Prime Mage Lockton that she should give her power away, it was time for her to prove to them all.

Prime Mage Lockton used the two blasphemous lessers as an example, she pulled every drop of liquid from their bodies and allowed the crowd of lesser mages to watch as the two bodies dried and shrivelled before their eyes.

Prime Mage Lockton ruled until the year 176 through regular reminders that she was indeed a God to the lesser mages. By this time however Prime Mage Lockton could feel her body beginning to betray her. When the lesser mages rallied against her, Prime Mage Lockton effortlessly destroyed hundreds more lesser mages before deciding to leave her corporeal form behind. She made the only ever recorded prophecy.

'There will be an All-Power that will rule Nerium for eternity, they will teach this world the meaning of fear.' Before leaving her body for all time.

Isabella Lockton did not die in the year 176. Isabella Lockton lives still."

Aaron looked up to the group. The four of them looked at each other in silence.

Finally, Ajit summed up everything Aaron was feeling with just two words. “Holy shit!”

15

After lessons one Friday Aaron was sat with Tala, Ajit, and Amelie under the shade of the tree, tiny green leaves beginning to sprout from its branches. Tala was sat next to him snuggling against his shoulder, Amelie and Ajit were laid staring at the sky a few metres away.

"We've been here a month already." Tala said absentmindedly.

"I know, it's gone by so fast." Amelie replied.

Ajit propped himself up on one elbow. "Yeah, I'm actually starting to like it here."

Aaron would have joined in with the conversation, he too found it difficult to believe it had already been a month and he was enjoying learning magic. But something was bothering him, he was not sure what it was, but something was wrong. Was that anger he was feeling?

"I like it better now that Flak has moved me to deflection with you three." Ajit continued.

Yes, it was definitely anger, not his own but someone was angry, someone close by, he could feel their anger emanating from somewhere.

"Well, you should have practiced when you said you were going to, you could have been doing deflection with us weeks ago." Amelie laughed.

The anger was moving, coming towards them. Someone was very angry, and they were getting closer.

“I know but…”

“Quiet!” Aaron said loudly, stopping their conversations. “Put your shields up.” He told them as he stood up and moved around the tree. He saw Dylan and three others walking towards him from the school, it was the first time he had seen him since the first day, when he had attacked him in the common room. Had he been in detention this whole time? “You three should go.” He said to Tala, Amelie, and Ajit.

“We aren’t going anywhere Aaron.” Amelie and Tala said together.

“I’m serious, you three aren’t as good at deflecting attacks as I am, you should go.” He said back to them.

“Not going to happen mate.” Ajit replied.

Aaron shook his head, Ajit had only just started to learn deflection two days before. Aaron could not be sure of what was about to happen, but from the amount of anger radiating from Dylan, he knew that it was not going to be good, and now he was going to be worried about keeping his friends safe as well as whatever Dylan and his group were going to do.

“You got me a month’s detention!” Dylan shouted at Aaron. “Do you know what detention is here?”

Aaron looked calmly back at him. "I didn't get you anything Dylan, you attacked me, remember."

"Detention here is sitting in a dark room with nothing, just food coming through a slot." Dylan continued, ignoring what Aaron had said. "You did that to me!" He screamed as he shot flames from his hands at Aaron, just as he had done on the day Aaron had first arrived.

Aaron raised one hand and effortlessly absorbed Dylan's attack. "Dylan, that didn't work when I'd had no training. What makes you think it will work out any differently now?" He was getting annoyed by this boy, he should do what Henry Carmine did and expand an air bubble inside the boys' brain and expand it until his head burst. Aaron shook the thought from his head.

"Because now I'm not on my own." Dylan replied smiling as one of his friends' lifted rocks from beneath him and shot them straight at Aarons head, screaming at the effort it took.

Aaron considered deflecting the stream of rocks back at his attackers for a moment, instead he just looked at the rocks as they flew toward him, and they fell back to the ground. "Come on, stop this or you'll all end up with Dylan in his dark room."

A strong wind erupted around Aaron and his friends, Aaron could see another of Dylan's friends with his arms outstretched pointed towards him. Aaron put his hands out to each side of him and the wind dispersed.

Dylan bared his teeth and snarled at his friends “Just get him!” And they all attacked together.

Jets of flames, streams of rocks, bolts of ice and shards of electricity shot towards Aaron. Once again Aaron thought about redirecting all of the attacks straight back at them, he imagined combining them to tear his attackers to shreds. Especially Dylan, he could use the rocks and ice to tear his flesh open and then send the electricity into the open wounds and fry him from the inside. Like the first time Dylan had attacked him, Aaron could imagine Dylan laying on the ground, this time his body torn open, he could see the electricity entering his open wounds, he could hear Dylan’s screams of pain. He shook his head to remove the thought and raised both arms above his head and brought them down together. The rocks fell to the ground, the flames met the ice and the two turned to steam, the electricity turned to nothing more than static and hung in the air.

“Just stop! There’s no need for this.” Aaron tried again to reason with them.

Dylan glared at him with his teeth bared, then his eyes flicked from Aaron to his friends. “Get his friends to split his focus.” He told his group.

"No!" Aaron screamed and whipped his arms around him lifting earth and rocks from the ground and moving them so that they surrounded him and his friends. He kept moving his arms building the giant shield thicker and thicker. Once he was happy with the earth shield, he did the same with an ice shield underneath, then there were two shields surrounding Aaron and his group, separating them from their attackers. Aaron could feel the attacks hit the earth shield, but nothing could make it through.

"Aaron, how are you doing this?" Tala's shocked voice came out of the darkness.

Aaron did not answer, keeping his concentration on the two shields protecting them. Aaron felt the attacks lessen then he heard muffled voices on the other side. The attacks stopped. Aaron waited for them to begin again but no more attacks came.

Instead, there came a gentle knock on the shield and then Head Mistress Taylors voice rang on the air inside. "Mr Scott, your attackers have been dealt with."

Unsure, Aaron thought of his friends, Tala in particular. He felt her hand gently lay on his arm and he began to lower the shields.

"Keep your air shields up for now." He told his friends. Once Aaron had dismantled both the earth and the ice shields, he saw two professors leading Dylan and his group away.

Head Mistress Taylor stood facing Aaron. “I apologise Mr Scott. Mr Lawson and his friends will be back in detention for quite a while. Is everyone ok? Does anyone need a Healer?”

Aaron looked to Tala, to Amelie and to Ajit. The three of them looking to each of their friends. Tala answered the head mistress. “We’re all fine, professor. None of their attacks got anywhere near us, thanks to Aaron.” She and the other two smiled at Aaron.

“Good.” The Head Mistress said, then she looked to Aaron. “How did you make that shield? As far as I know, no one has ever made a shield bigger than one person. You just created a perfect earth shield surrounding not just yourself but your three friends as well.”

“Not just an earth shield, he made one out of ice underneath it too.” Ajit said shakily.

“Why?” The head mistress asked Aaron.

“In case they managed to get through the first shield.” He looked directly at her. “I don’t know how I did it, head mistress. I heard Dylan tell his friends to attack these three to get to me.” He looked to his friends. “And I just had to keep them safe.”

Head Mistress Taylor looked at Aaron with her brows furrowed, “Why not just stop Mr Lawson and the others?”

"Stop them? I kept asking them to stop, they weren't really in the mood for chatting though. I had to protect my friends." He shot back at her.

"That's not what I meant."

"I know exactly what you meant." He interjected, getting annoyed. "You meant why didn't I return their attacks and kill them? I have no interest in that. I don't care that I'm an All-Power! I am not going to kill people!" He looked away from the head mistress, wondering about that moment where he wanted to tear them apart and fry Dylan from the inside, he shook his head. "All I wanted to do was protect my friends, to keep my friends safe and unharmed. Something that the older students here, clearly don't care about." He blurted out before he could stop himself. "Sorry head mistress." He added with a sigh.

The head mistress smiled and shook her head. "No need to apologise, Mr Scott. In fact, I'm glad you got angry when I suggested that. I am beyond happy that you chose to protect, rather than attack. I won't lie, I would love to know how you made a shield big enough for the four of you." She looked at the other three for a moment and ended the conversation. "I'll have some hot drinks sent out, you four rest up and try to enjoy the weekend." She turned and left.

Aaron turned to his friends again. "Are you sure you're all ok?"

Tala hugged him, Amelie ran her hands through her hair and Ajit dropped to the ground. “Physically, yes, we’re ok. Mentally, not so much, I nearly pissed my pants. That was scary as hell.” He said from the floor.

Amelie kicked his leg. “It was scary, but I’m not going to stop being your friend, before you say it.”

Aaron smiled and shook his head. “I wasn’t going to suggest it, I’d have had a terrible month if you three weren’t my friends.”

“I’m never leaving your side.” Tala said, still hugging Aaron.

“We already knew that, it didn’t take an attack for us to know that.” Ajit said from the ground. Amelie kicked him again, but this time she was laughing.

Aaron looked back towards the school while the other three continued chatting and laughing, he needed to find out how long they would be in detention for this time. So he could be ready for them the next time they tried to attack him.

16

After breakfast the next morning, the four of them were heading back to the tree, Ajit and Amelie walking a little ahead of Aaron and Tala.

Ajit turned back to Aaron. “You know, I get why the three of us like to come out here to relax, but why do you need to relax so much?” He asked as he walked backwards. “You don’t have as many classes as we do.”

Aaron was shocked, but he was also happy to see his shock mirrored in Tala and Amelie’s faces. “What do you mean? I’m learning every type of magic.”

“Yeah, but.” Ajit dismissed, waving his hands. “But you’ve got a free session nearly every day.”

“No, I haven’t.” Aaron answered, his shock at Ajit’s initial statement turning into confusion.

“You have, you know, those self study sessions.” He threw up air quotes when he said, ‘self study’. He smiled and added. “Self study sounds a lot like nap time to me.”

Aaron burst into laughter, finally figuring out that Ajit was not saying any of this to get at him. He was just being Ajit, the boy who chose not to practice, of course he would shy away from studying if he had an opportunity to.

“Maybe you’d have a nap, but I actually study. For the last few weeks, I haven’t been having any luck though.”

Tala looked up at him. “What do you mean? Have you been looking for something in particular?”

“Actually, yeah.” He nodded. “Ever since we read about Nicholas Garnier, I’ve been trying to find out how to meditate.”

“You idiot.” Ajit laughed loudly. “You should have just asked! I was raised Hindu. I know how to meditate.” He continued to laugh, shaking his head at Aaron.

Aaron did feel like an idiot. “You can? Can you teach me?”

“Whoa, whoa, whoa. Stop!” Amelie interrupted, raising her hands. “Why do you want to know how to meditate? According to your book, Garnier used meditation to speak with Lockton. Why would you want to talk to her?”

Aaron looked at her for a moment. “You remember that weird dream I had?” He asked her with a sigh. She nodded. “It wasn’t the first one, I’d had another one before that. I’d gone full bad guy, I even had a throne. You and Tala were kind of like my generals and.” He looked at Ajit and decided to change the dream a little. “You were fighting against us.”

Amelie shook her head, her face reddening. “You’re willing to talk to the biggest wacko ever on Nerium because you had some dreams? Aaron, you can’t risk talking to that nutjob, because of some dreams.”

“They were more than dreams, they felt real Amelie.” He tried to explain to her.

“They were just dreams, Aaron.” She interrupted, almost shouting at him now. “You can’t risk speaking to that maniac for some dreams.” She continued, hardly listening to what Aaron was trying to tell her.

Tala walked to her and took hold of her hand. “Let’s go for a walk Amelie.”

“No! We can’t let him.”

“Amelie! Walk! Now!” Tala interrupted her and dragged her away, looking back with a raised eyebrow at Aaron as she went.

Aaron nodded at her, giving her permission to tell Amelie the real first dream.

“So, can you teach me?” Aaron asked Ajit as soon as the girls were out of earshot.

Ajit nodded. “Of course, but, are you sure you want to talk to her. Amelie’s got a point, the woman thought she was a god.”

“It’s not so much her I want to talk to.” Aaron admitted. “I’m hoping that they’re all there. I’m hoping I can talk to others, Aban Fasil to be honest. Maybe one of them knows about the dreams.”

"OK." Ajit said, giving in. "The way we do it is we sit alone and repeat a mantra in Sanskrit in our heads, that might not be the best way for you though. What you could try is still sitting alone somewhere quiet and comfortable, not too bright, not too dark. To start with don't do it for too long, start short and build up over time. Concentrate on your breathing, some people will tell you to clear your mind, you can't do that, your mind is always going to wander. When it does wander, bring your attention back to your breathing. When your mind wanders don't try to analyse your thoughts just get your attention back to your breathing. With enough practice, your mind should start to relax, and you should go into kind of like a trance." He looked at Aaron. "It's pretty simple really. Just takes quite a bit of practice, I'll help you."

Aaron could not believe it, for weeks he had been scouring his books, searching for information and Ajit could have told him how to do it, if he had only thought to ask.

"Thank you, Ajit." He shook his head and let out a relieved sigh. "I've wasted weeks reading all sorts of crap, when I could have just asked you." He laughed. "Shall we go and get the girls before Amelie starts shouting again?" He said as he nodded towards where Tala and Amelie were stood, the latter staring at them.

Ajit laughed and the two set off towards them. "I don't mind as long as she's shouting at you, and not me."

"When are you going to make a move on her? It's obvious you like each other." Aaron asked him.

Ajit playfully bumped into him with his shoulder, knocking him slightly off balance. “You can’t talk, what about you and Tala? All the two of you have done is hold hands.” He laughed a little and added with a whisper as they got close to the girls. “I will when you do.”

Aaron smiled shaking his head at him. Then he saw Amelie’s face, he stopped smiling. “Everything Ok?”

“Can we talk?” She asked glaring at him.

“OK, we’ll go back to the tree.” He answered a little sheepishly.

“Nope.” Tala interrupted, shaking her head at the two of them. “Me and Ajit will go back to the tree, and we’ll relax, you two can talk and then join us when you’re done and you’re ready to chill out a bit.”

“Ok.” Aaron and Amelie said together and watched as Tala and Ajit wandered away.

“How could you not tell me!?” Amelie exclaimed as soon as the others were back at the tree.

“I didn’t even want to tell Tala to begin with, she made me tell her.” He admitted. “She’s a little scary when she gets bossy.” Amelie nodded and let out a small chuckle. “Being serious though. I am sure these are more than just dreams. What did Tala tell you?”

She shrugged. “Just that Ajit died, and you wanted to find out if it’s going to happen so you can stop it.”

Aaron took a breath and told her every detail of the first dream, it was easy to do. The whole thing was still etched in his mind.

“Oh god!” She gasped clasping her hands to her mouth.

“He didn’t just die, Amelie. I murdered him. You and Tala handed out the sentence and I murdered him. But it’s not just that, it made me happy. Murdering my friend made me happy.” He looked at her for a moment. “I need to know if that was just a dream or if any part of it was any kind of prophecy. I cannot let that happen to my friend, I just can’t Amelie.”

She wiped a tear from her eye and looked toward the tree. “Ok, but I’m still mad at Tala.” The two of them set off back to the tree. “We live in the same room, we talk about all sorts of stuff before we go to sleep, and she didn’t mention anything.”

“I made her promise not to say anything about it to anyone, and I’ll ask for the same promise from you. Please, don’t tell your boyfriend that I murdered him.” He said attempting to shock her into forgetting to be mad at Tala.

“My boyfriend?” It worked. Aaron smiled at her. “What? He’s not my boyfriend, nothing like that.” She argued, but she was beginning to blush.

“Come on, you two like each other. It’s obvious.” He pushed.

"Just, shut up." She said as they reached the tree.

17

The following Friday, Aaron had just left Tala and the other dual mages after History of Nerium, which in Aaron's opinion was much more boring now that all they learnt about was the founding of settlements and villages in the early days of Nerium. He was on his way to Head Mistress Taylors office for his fifth weekly interview, she was going to want to talk about the attack again, he knew it.

He knocked on the door and heard the head mistress's voice telling him to come in but was surprised to see a man he did not know when he entered. The head mistress and the man were sat in two of the three armchairs surrounding the fire in the office. Half expecting another attack, Aaron stayed standing nervously in the open doorway, waiting for the head mistress to introduce the man.

"Mr Scott, this is Prime Mage Reid." Head Mistress Taylor finally said to Aaron.

Prime Mage Reid stood up and held out a hand to Aaron. "Please, it's Jason."

Aaron observed him for a moment then took a few cautious steps toward him and shook his hand. "Aaron." He introduced himself, pointlessly as the Prime Mage obviously knew his name already.

The Prime Mage sat back down and gestured to the only empty armchair in the office, he watched as Aaron sat down and sat staring at him with a forced smile on his face.

Aaron was not sure what to think of the Prime Mage, to be on the safe side and without moving he slowly built an air shield around him. He saw Head Mistress Taylor hide a smile behind her hand, he got the feeling that she could see his shield as he built it.

"Aaron, can I call you Aaron?" The Prime Mage began, he looked to Aaron but continued before he could respond. "As you know, The Head Mistress here has kept me up to date with your progress." He paused to smile at Head Mistress Taylor. "You are learning at an exceptional rate, you are courteous to your professors, and you are making friends. This is all good. Or it would be if you were a normal student." His forced smile faltered. "But you are not a normal student, are you? Given the history of your kind, I find this very troubling." His smile faded away.

"My kind?" Aaron asked with a raised eyebrow, this man was already irritating him.

"Yes Aaron, your kind. There is not one single All-Power that hasn't been evil, I am yet to receive information that will convince me that you are any different."

Aaron listened to the Prime Mage, feeling anger build within him.

"You are learning at an exceptional rate, to me that says you are, or you will become, very powerful. You are courteous to your professors, to me that says you are intentionally trying to make them think you are a half decent person. You are making friends, that could be the beginning of an actual army."

This man is pathetic, Aaron thought as he worked hard not to let any anger show. He was going out of his way to prove Aaron was a threat.

"If there was a way to send you back to Earth, I would have sent you back already." The Prime Mage continued, his forced smile reappeared on his face. "Of course, it has only been five weeks since your emergence and you have not yet broken any rules." He dropped his smile once more. "Be assured however, the moment you do, I and my forces will be there to stop you."

I'd like to see you try, Aaron couldn't help but think. This man was nothing more than a bully.

The Prime Mage stood up and the forced smile was back once more. "Now, I am a very busy man so I will take my leave. Good day Head Mistress. Aaron." He nodded to each in turn and went to walk out of the office.

Aaron had had many ‘one way conversations’ while he had been in the Army on Earth. But he was not going to let this power hungry little man speak to him like that, he did not stand for bullies. He tried hard to get rid of thoughts about ripping the Prime Mage limb from limb and tried even harder not to let his anger show through his voice.

“We will never know if you are wrong Jason.” Aaron said before the Prime Mage got to the door.

The Prime Mage turned back to him, his lips pursed angrily. “I believe you mean ‘Prime’ don’t you?”

Aaron nodded. “That is exactly what I would have called you, until you said ‘please, call me Jason’. But like I said, we can never know if you’re wrong. Aban Fasil could have been a good man if it wasn’t for Anastasia Solovyov’s influence. I’m sure you know that there is absolutely no evidence that he ever harmed another mage, yes, he was complicit, but we cannot know if that was his choice or her influence.”

The Prime Mage opened his mouth to argue, but Aaron barrelled on.

"Then there is Nicholas Garnier, he never even had a chance to choose for himself did he Jason." The Prime Mage flinched angrily as Aaron used his first name again. "Is that what you would like to do to me? Chain me up in the main hall? Leave me there until I starve to death?" He paused as though he was giving the Prime an opportunity to answer, but continued before he could speak again. "Head Mistress Taylor has been keeping you informed of what I have been doing here at Doctrina, so I am sure you know about the two unprovoked attacks against me. And as you know about those, I am sure you know that I survived the first one on instinct alone and the second, I did everything I could to protect my friends instead of raising a finger against our attackers." Aaron paused to take a breath, noticing the tiniest look of surprise on the Prime Mages face, confirming his suspicions that he had not read the head mistress's reports, or at least not fully read them.

"Now Jason, please don't take this outburst as an indication that I am evil." He continued, intentionally using his first name again to annoy him. "Instead, please know that this is exactly how I would have reacted back on Earth when faced with your kind of intolerance. Just because someone is different to you, that does not give you the right to persecute them." Aaron looked away from the Prime Mage but carried on talking. "I'm not disagreeing that 'most' All-Powers have been bad, but I do think you might be overlooking something." He looked back at the Prime, finally giving him a chance to answer.

"Really? And what might that be?" He answered through his clenched teeth, not bothering to hide his anger.

"The last time an All-Power arrived, Alexander Miller, was before Prime Mage Proctor did whatever she did to allow people to live a full life before being brought here." Aaron continued, doing a much better job of hiding his anger than the Prime Mage was. "I am the first All-Power to get here that isn't an actual teenager, regardless of how I look, meaning that my mind is not as susceptible as the rest of them." Aaron could tell from the Primes face that he had not considered this. "If you had bothered to actually read Head Mistress Taylors reports on me, you would know that I spent almost all my adult life fighting against bullies like you, fighting for equal treatment and teaching people that diversity can be a good thing."

The Prime Mage stood chewing the insides of his cheek for a moment. "I will be watching you carefully Mr Scott."

"I would expect nothing less. Prime Mage." Aaron spat out his title. "Only this time, perhaps you could actually read Head Mistress Taylors reports on me."

The Prime Mage turned and left the office, slamming the door behind him. Aaron turned to Head Mistress Taylor to see her holding a finger in the air to keep him quiet. She sat there looking at the door until they heard the Prime Mages footsteps going down the corridor. She let out a breath when she was sure he had left. "I had a feeling he was going to be like that. Like I said to you the first time we spoke, it is going to be up to us to change everyone's minds about you. But you handled him admirably."

Aaron shook his head and asked. "Is he always like that?"

"I am afraid he has given in to his fear of All-Powers since your arrival." She smiled sadly at him. "I have already given him my 'report' for this week, so I won't keep you in here much longer, just long enough to make sure the Prime Mage has left the grounds."

"You really said all that to the Prime Mage?" Amelie said that evening, they were all sat in Aarons room. Aaron had just finished telling them all about his meeting with the Prime.

"Yeah, the man is nothing more than a bully. I just couldn't stand it." He answered her as he paced around his library, the anger that he had felt toward the Prime Mage still bubbling within him. "I've only been here just over a month, and he's decided that I'm bad news just because I'm an All-Power, he basically told me he was forming an army to bring me down."

"Really?" Tala asked. "Are you sure?"

"He said 'I and my forces will be there to stop you.' What does that sound like to you?" He shook his head. "I was hoping that the professors were exaggerating."

"You can't really blame him though." Ajit said. "I don't agree with him." He added quickly when he saw Aaron's face. "It's just that they've all been taught that every All-Power was evil. Not one of them has ever been taught that any All-Power had any redeeming qualities. He's scared."

"Don't you think I'm scared?" Aaron shot back at him. "Six weeks ago, I was getting on with a normal life, I had normal worries, like 'am I going to have a job next month'. Now here I am with a whole world against me with worries like 'who's going to try to kill me next'. Don't you think I'm scared?"

"I don't agree with him, I said that. I'm just trying to think the way he's thinking." Ajit said back. "Wait, you're scared?"

Aaron didn't answer, he just stared at Ajit for a minute before Ajit turned away. Aaron immediately felt bad for getting mad at him. "Ajit, I'm sorry, I'm still angry because of the Prime Mage, I shouldn't take it out on you. I know you don't think like that."

Ajit just nodded but said nothing more, Amelie sat with him, but she did not say anything either. Aaron looked at Tala, she smiled sadly at him and then Aaron heard her say.

"You're scared? I didn't know you was scared. I wish I could help you."

But she had not said it, her mouth had not moved, she still had that sad smile on her face. Aaron had heard her voice, and her words but inside his head.

"What's wrong?" She said, noticing the confused look on his face.

"I, er…" He looked at the other two. "Nothing."

Amelie looked between Tala and Aaron then said to Ajit. “Let’s give these two some alone time.” Clearly getting the wrong idea but Aaron didn’t mind. He could tell Tala what he had just heard and find out if it was something to do with being an All-Power or if he was going mad. Ajit gave Aaron a small smile as he and Amelie left.

Tala hardly waited for the door to close. “Spill it! Whatever just happened, you have to tell me.”

Aaron couldn’t help but smile at her, the anger within him seeming to evaporate as he sat down next to her. “You’re brilliant, you know that right?”

“Yes, I do know that, took you long enough to figure it out.” She chuckled. “But that’s not what just happened. Stop trying to change the subject. Tell me.”

“Ok, I’m either going nuts or, I don’t know what.” He said shaking his head. “Just then, when I looked at you, I heard your voice in my head.”

She looked as though she did not believe him, of course not, why would she. “What did I say?”

“You said ‘You’re scared? I didn’t know you was scared. I wish I could help you.’ Those exact words, that’s it.”

Tala's jaw nearly hit the floor. "I was thinking about saying that to you when you suddenly looked scared and confused." She stood up and started pacing round his sofa. "What does this mean? Can you read minds now? Oh my god! If you can't figure out how to control that, you will definitely go nuts, it'll be like everyone is screaming at you all the time."

She kept talking and pacing round Aaron's library until Aaron stood up and grabbed her by the shoulders. "Tala, calm down, I don't think I can read minds. I think it's something else, something I've read about."

"Are you reading my mind right now?" She asked him as she looked up into his eyes, her voice barely more than a whisper. He noticed he was still holding her by her shoulders.

He let go. "No." He said smiling at her.

She let out a disappointed breath and moved away to sit on the sofa again. "Ok. What have you read about?"

Aaron took a book from the shelf, looked at his armchair and then moved to sit next to her on the sofa. "Have you got this book in your room?" He showed her *Notable All-Power abilities uncommon in other Mages*. She shook her head. "There's a piece on Aban Fasil and Anastasia Solovyov. You see, even though she was killing for one hundred and fifteen years. They were doing it quietly. So, the two still had a life and they were liked in their own community." He said as he looked through the book trying to find the right page. "Got it, here, listen to this.

Aban Fasil and Anastasia Solovyov were seen to have an unspoken link, almost as though they could speak to and communicate with each other within their minds. They were also observed communicating while in different areas.

This is an ability unseen in any other mage, it has been theorised that the two had a strong emotional bond which allowed them to speak telepathically, although it is not known how this can be performed or if it can be learnt by other mages.

That's what I think this could be. Either that or I am actually going nuts." He looked up from the book and noticed Tala staring at him. "I think I heard that because you wanted to say it to me."

"You think we have an emotional bond?" She said quietly, a smile spreading across her face.

"Really? Telepathic communication and that's what you take?" He sighed, but he was smiling. "Tala, last week I created a shield that apparently no one else has ever done because I care about all three of you. And it's no real secret that I care about you most." He looked her in the eyes and thought *'All we need to do is learn how to do it on purpose.'* She showed no signs that she had heard him. He sighed and was about to look away.

Then he heard her voice in his head again. *'Kiss me.'*

He smiled again. "I heard that."

“Heard what?” She said quietly.

He kissed her.

Over that weekend, Aaron and Tala tried everything they could think of, by Sunday Aaron could hear Tala whenever she wanted to talk to him. But she was yet to hear him, until Sunday afternoon.

The four of them were in the Air Fire Classroom. Aaron had promised them all that he would try and help them get their shields to the point where they could glide like he could.

“All I did was try to extend the shield under my feet as well as around me.” Aaron demonstrated by creating his own shield and lifting himself off the ground. “When you do it, it doesn’t feel like you’re flying or anything like that. It just feels like you’re standing on the floor.” He was saying to Amelie when Tala’s voice rang inside his head. Aaron was by no means innocent but what she said made him blush and drop back to the ground. *‘Oh my god Tala!’* He thought, not expecting her to hear it.

But he heard her squeal from the other side of the classroom, out loud. Amelie and Ajit heard her as well. They all turned to look at her, she saw them all staring. “Sorry, I thought I did it. I got a bit scared.” She lied. *‘I heard you, you said oh my god.’* she sent into Aaron’s head.

‘You did?’ He thought back to her. She nodded, he smiled. *‘This is brilliant.’*

18

Weeks passed and Aaron was grateful that he had had no new dreams, at the same time he was also a little disheartened that he had not had much progress with meditation. He had found it difficult to begin with, until he remembered how calming he used to find the ticking of a clock, there were no clocks on Nerium, but he found that just imagining the ticks and the tocks while he was meditating helped. He could now meditate for nearly an hour each time. But still nothing when it came to speaking to All-Powers of the past.

Dylan and his friends had finished their detentions but had decided not to attack him again. “This isn’t over, I will stop you.” Dylan had said when he had first appeared back in the common room. “But I will not let you put me back in detention. You better be able to see out of the back of your head All-Power.”

Aaron had done nothing but smile at him when he had said that. Aaron did not need to see him, he could feel Dylan’s anger before he could reach Aaron with his magic.

Tala and Aaron could communicate telepathically from opposite ends of the school. That had slowed both of their learning for a few weeks, as the two of them were speaking to each other for hours every night and neglecting their studies. Tala had put a stop to that when Ajit began to surpass her in their dual lessons.

Amelie had perfected her sphere shield, that is what they had decided to call the shield that lifted them off the ground as no one other than Aaron had ever done it, and Tala was not far behind.

Aaron had moved on from deflection to control of each of the main elements in all of his dual classes, in his healing class he had progressed farther than anyone, to the point where he had even assisted Professor Iaso when six of the second year Fire mages had been brought to her classroom, each with severe burns after they had momentarily forgotten how to deflect, while they were learning how to direct their fire streams.

Before he knew it two more months had passed, and they had arrived at their first break in learning. The first and second year professors remained in the school while the third and fourth year professors took their students on a short tour of Nerium.

“It’s because most of us leave after three years, the professors show us round villages and towns to give us an idea of where to go after we finish school.” Heidi had told Aaron when he had asked her about it.

“It’s nice and quiet without the third years.” Ajit remarked after the Spring celebration feast, the four of them were sat lazily in the common room, their bellies full.

“And the fourth years. They’ve gone as well.” Amelie added.

Ajit shrugged that off. “They don’t count, there’s only six of them.”

“They should count, we’ll be the fourth years one day. I bet you won’t say we don’t count when we’re in our fourth year.”

The two of them continued to chat like that while Tala and Aaron watched them as though they were watching a tennis match. “Hey, can you show us what you’ve been doing in class?” Tala asked Aaron.

“Yeah, we can go and practice in the classroom tomorrow.” He answered, happy that she had asked out loud rather than in his head. He had started to get a little bored of listening to Amelie and Ajit.

“Yeah, you could teach us to do it too.” Ajit added.

Aaron shook his head. “You still haven’t got deflection nailed. And I’m already trying to teach you to do the sphere shield.”

Ajit slumped in his chair. “But I can’t do that.”

Amelie punched him in the shoulder. “You are not giving up to just try something new. Besides we’ll move onto doing what Aaron is doing soon enough.”

The evening dragged on with more small talk, Ajit complaining about not being as good as Tala and Amelie, Amelie pointing out that he would be if he actually practiced with them. Until Ajit stood up and declared he was going to bed.

"It is getting late." Amelie agreed as she stood. "Are you coming?" She asked Tala.

"Not just yet." Tala replied, smiling at her.

Amelie looked between her and Aaron with a smirk on her face. "OK." She turned and started to walk away. "Have fun." She shouted back over her shoulder.

Tala waited until the two of them had gone into the Air Fire mage corridor then she turned to Aaron. "So, how comfy is that big bed of yours?"

*

Aaron was in a circular room he did not recognise, there was one door and no windows, no tables, and no desks, but there were paintings on the walls, eight of them, with one of the smokeless torches between each of them.

Something about the paintings felt a little off to him. He moved to the closest one, it was a painting of a regal looking elderly woman, a small plaque underneath the frame read 'Isabella Lockton'. Aaron went from painting to painting, memorising the faces of each All-Power that came before him.

It was only after looking at Alexander Millers painting that he realised what was wrong, Aaron was the seventh All-Power to arrive on Nerium, but here, in this room there were eight paintings.

Aaron stood in front of the painting between Alexander Miller and a painting of himself. The painting in front of him showed only a silhouette, Aaron could not make out any details, he could not tell if it was a painting of a man or a woman, whether they were young or old, there was no way Aaron could tell. The plaque underneath was completely blank. Unsure what to make of it he turned toward the door to leave.

“I’m not certain you want to leave just yet.” A deep voice came from the centre of the room.

Aaron turned to see a man stood in front of him, a man he recognised from one of the paintings. Aban Fasil was stood in front of him. “How is this possible?” Aaron asked him.

Aban just smiled. “It’s a dream, anything is possible in a dream.”

“I know it’s a dream, it feels like the others.” Aaron answered. “Does this mean that the other two dreams I’ve had like this one were just dreams?”

“How should I know?” Aban shrugged, his smile beginning to irritate Aaron. “I’m part of your dream, I only know what you know.” He said, still with that irritating smile on his face. Aaron shook his head and turned to leave again.

"But perhaps you know more than you realise." Aaron turned back but didn't say anything to him. "Perhaps the reason that I am here in your dream is because, out of all of the All-powers on these paintings, I am the one that spent the longest in this school." He saw Aarons confused look and he gestured to the room. "Yes, we are still at Doctrina. You know that Isabella Lockton built this school, what you have figured out but perhaps not realised that you have figured out. Is that she made the school give preferential treatment to All-Powers." He made a motion as if he was pulling a chair out from under a table and a stiff wooden chair appeared in his hand and he sat down.

Aaron was getting more and more irritated by his smiling face and vague answers, he made the same motion and conjured a very comfortable looking armchair.

"More preferential treatment to some than others, it would seem." Aban continued as he looked at Aarons chair. "Regardless, this is a room within the school. Hidden to all but All-Powers, I am certain there are others, but I was unable to find any in my time as a student, or as a professor." He waited, expecting Aaron to ask a question, when he didn't, Aban continued. "In some deep dark part of your mind you have also realised, but perhaps not noticed that you have realised, that in your two previous dreams you showed certain abilities. Your brain knows how to do those magics."

Suddenly Aaron was not irritated by Aban's smile anymore. "So, if I were to attempt those abilities when I was awake, I would know if my dreams were real or not?"

“That, is not what I am saying, if you were to try those magics while you were awake all you would have to do is think about how you did them in the dreams and, perhaps, you would be able to do them.” He studied Aaron for a moment. “I am not saying that your dreams were prophecy, perhaps not 100% prophecy at least. Example, why would you kill one of your best friends? Especially when he looked exactly as he does now. If he looked forty or fifty years older, then it could almost be understandable, perhaps you did go bad, and he had spent decades fighting against you. But he did not look forty or fifty years older, did he? No. So why would you kill him? Answer, you wouldn’t. Perhaps your act of murder is not the point you should focus on.”

“So, what should I focus on?” Aaron asked, sitting forward in his armchair.

Aban yawned and dropped his smile. “I’m bored now. Wake up.”

*

Aaron sat up in his bed hardly able to digest what he had just seen and heard.

“What is it? Did you have another dream?” Tala’s sleepy voice came from next to him.

He looked at her, smiled and laid back down. “Yes, but nothing to worry about, I’ll tell you about it in the morning.” But she had already gone back to sleep.

As he laid there next to her, he thought about what Aban had just said and about what he had already learnt from his professors. He could not practice opening a doorway here in his room, at least not while Tala was sleeping next to him, that left the spike, the murder weapon from his first dream. Professor Flak had taught him how to control his air magic to the point where he could create a small tornado in his hand, but that was far from what he had done in the dream. He held his hand out next to him, palm facing up and thought about what he had done in the dream, instantly he felt the air above his hand harden into a long spike. He concentrated more and the spike turned into a circular band which he was able to shrink and expand. Exactly how he had killed Ajit in his dream. Aaron laid there awake for the rest of the night.

19

Ajit and Amelie were already in the main hall having breakfast when Aaron and Tala walked in the next morning. Ajit looked up at the two of them when they got to the table. "You look exhausted mate." He said to Aaron.

"I didn't get much sleep." He replied, yawning, and rubbing his eyes.

Amelie tried unsuccessfully not to laugh and ended up spitting juice all over her breakfast. "Not like that." Tala said, rolling her eyes. "He had another dream." She sat next to Amelie and quietly added. "Maybe a little bit like that though." The two of them starting to giggle like actual schoolgirls.

"How do you know he had another dream?" Ajit asked. "Wait, don't you two normally come to breakfast together?" He added pointing between Tala and Amelie." Then realisation lit his eyes. "Were you two together last night?" Aaron and Tala just smiled at him. "When did this happen? I swear, nobody tells me anything."

"You are just oblivious to everything aren't you." Amelie said smiling at him. "They've been together for months." She turned to Aaron. "What terrifying thing did you dream this time?"

“Actually, nothing terrifying this time.” He went on and told them about his latest dream, conveniently forgetting about the conversation about him murdering Ajit and neglecting to mention that he had been able to create the very same murder weapon out of thin air.

“Secret All-Power rooms in the school. I suppose there could be, the school definitely likes you, seeing how much better your room is compared to ours.” Amelie said almost to herself.

“Oh, his bath is amazing. You have to try it.” Tala said leaning into Amelie, the pair of them starting to giggle again.

“Why are we going to practice in the classroom again? Don’t we have two weeks off from learning?” Ajit complained as they walked the corridors after breakfast.

He was walking with Aaron, the two girls walking a little ahead of them talking to each other in hushed tones and occasionally glancing back. “To practice, isn’t it obvious.” Aaron laughed. “Are you two sure you can’t wait to gossip until you’re alone?” He shouted ahead.

“No, I need to know now.” Amelie shouted back with a smile.

Aaron shook his head, Ajit laughed and bumped into him. “Surely you know by now that women talk.”

“Yeah, but I wouldn’t mind not hearing them laugh and giggle about it.” Aaron answered glumly.

“They aren’t laughing at you mate.” Ajit said, more serious than he had been for a while. “Look at her.” He nodded towards Tala. “She’s beaming, I haven’t seen her that happy since we got here. And that girl is always happy.” He looked back at Aaron and noticed him smiling. “I’m not completely oblivious all the time.” He smiled and bumped into Aaron again. “So, what was it like?”

Aaron forced his gaze away from Tala. “We are absolutely not talking about it.”

“Ouch! That bad?” Ajit answered sarcastically.

“What, no, shut up.” Aaron laughed at him. “I’ll tell you what we can talk about though.” He said smiling. “What was it you said.” He paused, tapping his finger against his chin. “Hmm, oh yes that was it. You said, ‘I will when you do.’ I made my move months ago, we just decided to keep it quiet. Its time you made your move before you’re permanently in the friendzone.”

Ajit’s eyes widened and he went pale. “What? No, I didn’t mean it. We, we’re just friends.” He stammered as he looked at Amelie walking ahead of them and frowned. “I don’t know if I can, maybe it’s already too late.” He admitted. “Anyway, if you two decided to keep it quiet, how come Amelie knew already?”

Aaron bumped his shoulder into him. “Surely you know by now that women talk.” Ajit rolled his eyes and the two of them were laughing when they walked into the Air Fire Classroom.

"What are you two laughing at?" Amelie asked as soon as she heard them.

Ajit worriedly looked to Aaron. "Nothing you need to worry about." Aaron answered her and Ajit let out a breath. Aaron looked across the large classroom. "I'm going over there for a moment, wait here, I'll be right back." He started walking to the other side of the room, whispering to Ajit on his way past him. "Tick tock my friend."

Once he was on the other side of the room, he thought about what he had done in his second dream. In his dream all he had done was think about walking through a doorway into his office, and a green door had opened in front of him. "It can't be that simple. Can it?" He said to himself, but he tried anyway. He thought about taking a step through an imaginary door that led back to the other side of the room, a door that led back to his friends, a door that led back to Tala. A rectangle of green light appeared in front of him, and he stepped through, instantly appearing right next to Tala. "Holy shit! It worked." He laughed.

The other three stared at him in stunned silence for a moment, he looked from one to another, waiting for someone to say something. When no one did, he decided to try the last piece of magic he had done in a dream and technically should not know how to do. He put his hand out and felt the air beneath his palm harden and shape, he grabbed hold of that shape and pulled back, giving the hardened air texture and colour as he did. He sat on the new chair and waited for someone to say something.

“Are you kidding me!” Ajit shouted loudly, making the two girls jump. “You have to have practiced all of that, there’s no way you just opened a portal on your first try. Or, or made a chair out of nothing!”

“That’s just it, it’s what Aban was trying to tell me last night in my dream. This wasn’t my first try.” They all looked confused. “Last night I made a chair, and I made a better chair than Aban because he was annoying me. My brain remembered how to do it.” None of them looked convinced. “And in the dream where I was a professor, I was thirty years older than I am now. I opened a portal or a door or whatever that was, easily. So, in the dream I must have been doing it for years, and my brain remembered how to do it. In the dreams I did it all so easily, I don’t know, maybe it’s like muscle memory.” They were still staring at him. “And I didn’t make the chair out of nothing, I hardened the air and gave it texture and colour so it would be visible.” He smiled trying to make it sound less than it was.

“So, you made a chair out of thin air.” Ajit threw his hands into the air. “Yeah, that makes more sense.” He said as he started to pace back and forth.

“None of this makes sense.” Aaron admitted. “I don’t know how I can suddenly do magic that I did in a dream. I still don’t understand how each year for 763 years one hundred people have died on Earth and woken up here with magic powers, are you saying that that makes more sense than any of this?” Nobody answered him. “All I know is that I can somehow do magic that I have done in my dreams, that ridiculous explanation of my brain remembering how to do it, is the only thing I can think of.”

“Ok, Ok.” Amelie finally joined in. “For whatever reason, you can do these things that you knew how to do in dreams.” She shook her head in amazement. “Any other fantastic abilities?”

Aaron looked at her for a moment. *‘I think we should tell them.’* He thought to Tala. She looked worried for a moment but then nodded her head. Aaron stood up, the chair evaporating back into the air as he did. “Actually, yes.” He admitted. “I have a book called *Notable All-Power abilities uncommon in other Mages.* In that book it speaks about Aban Fasil and Anastasia Solovyov, when they were secretly killing, they had a life back in their local village and they were seen to communicate with each other. Telepathically.” He looked at the three of them. “A few months ago. Completely accidentally.” He paused, preparing himself for the reaction he knew was about to come. “Tala and I found out we could do it too.”

“Bullshit!” Shouted Ajit.

“What!” Amelie shouted whirling to Tala.

"It came out of nowhere one day, all of a sudden he could hear me when I wanted to talk to him." Tala burst out apologetically to Amelie. "And then after a few days practice, I could hear him too. And we could talk to each other all the time. And we didn't understand it, but it was kind of nice, like being back on Earth and having our phones back." She rambled on.

"We didn't tell either of you because it was so strange." Aaron interrupted, giving Tala chance to take a breath. "Like I said the book is called *Notable ALL-POWER abilities uncommon in other Mages.*"

"I don't believe it. You're going to have to prove that one." Ajit said, shaking his head with his eyes closed. "Nope, I don't believe it."

"Alright, fine. Go over there with Tala and say something to her, something that I wouldn't be able to guess. I'll shout it back to you from here." Ajit and Tala walked to the opposite wall and Ajit whispered something to Tala. A few moments later Aaron heard her repeat it inside his head. "Are you serious? You really want me to repeat that?" He shouted across the room.

Ajit held his arms out beside him. "You're full of crap, I don't believe you." He shouted back.

"Fine." Aaron shouted and continued. "I wish I could declare my feelings for Amelie like I was in a Bollywood movie."

Ajit dropped his arms to his sides. On the other side of the room, Aaron and Amelie heard his voice quietly say. "Shit."

Aaron looked to Amelie. "Do you believe me?"

"I had an idea anyway." She admitted, her eyes not leaving Ajit as he walked head bowed back to them. "For weeks, Tala would stare off into space and suddenly start laughing. I was about to ask her if that was when she was talking to you when she started ranting." She took her eyes off Ajit and looked at Aaron. "Did you know he liked me?"

"Of course I did, and I know you like him too. I tried to get you both to admit it months ago." He said quickly as Tala and Ajit were getting close.

Amelie walked up to Ajit as he got back to them and linked her arm in his, when he still didn't lift his head, she gave him a small kiss on his cheek. That brightened him up a little. "Do you think you could teach us how to do that?" She asked Aaron.

"Hold on." Ajit said, finally lifting his head. "If that's a side effect from sleeping with you. I don't want it." Tala blushed and buried her head in her hands. Amelie punched Ajit in his shoulder.

"You don't know what you're missing mate." Aaron laughed giving Ajit a wink. Tala punched him in his shoulder.

20

The four of them spent a lot of time practicing in the Air Fire Classroom over the Spring Celebration break, Tala and Ajit had both managed to do a full sphere shield. That made Aaron very happy, he saw that as confirmation that not everything in his dreams could be true. In his second dream, when he had read his chapter in *An accurate history of The All-Power* it had said;

Aaron Scott was extremely powerful, learning quickly and even teaching two dual mages things that no other dual mage had ever achieved.

Two dual mages, not three. Aaron had initially connected that with his first dream where Amelie and Tala were gliding alongside him. But, thanks to Aarons help, Amelie, Tala and now Ajit had all now perfected their sphere shields. All three of them.

Aaron had not performed any of the magics he had done from his dreams again. He felt that as he knew how to do them so well in the dreams, and the fact that he had done each with such ease while awake, his time would be better spent practicing what the professors were teaching him. This did not sit well with Ajit.

"We could go from your room to the main hall with one step." He had said when Aaron had told him he was going to practice his school magic. Or. "Why do we even have to go to the main hall? You could make food like you made the chair."
Aaron couldn't help but laugh when he had said that. "I probably could, but, like you said. I made the chair out of thin air. We would be eating air."

"Oh." Ajit had finally accepted that Aaron was not going to use those abilities unless he needed them. But he still complained every time they walked from the main hall to practice in the Air Fire Classroom.

At the halfway point of their break, Aaron was able to control each element so well that he could create miniature dragons and have them fly around his head. This was what he was doing in the Air Fire Classroom, he had a dragon of ice and one of fire flying around his head while he made a third of earth and a fourth of air, one in each hand. Once they were done, he set them off flying as well, he brought all four tiny dragons round to hover in front of his face, he spent a moment admiring his work. Then cocked his head to one side as a thought occurred to him.

"I wonder." He quietly spoke to himself.

He slowly moved the Fire and the Earth dragons together, instead of making them crash into each other, he combined the two. Making what looked like a dragon made from molten lava twice the size of the remaining two.

He smiled and moved the ice dragon toward it, slowly and carefully he combined them. He strengthened the ice to make sure it would not melt, and carefully placed it where he wanted it within the new dragon. Soon there was a lava dragon the size of a small dog with bright diamond like eyes in its face and spikes running down its back and tail.

Finally, he moved the air dragon in and combined the last one, the dragons' wings were now made out of visible wind, and it breathed out sparks of electricity from its nose. He admired his work a moment longer and sent his creation flying around the room, feeling the air rush over his own body, as though it was him that was soaring through the air. He closed his eyes and continued to control his creation, finding that he could see through its icy eyes. He flew the dragon passed his own body and saw himself smiling, he also noticed Amelie staring at him with a look of mixed concentration and pain on her face.

Aaron opened his eyes and dropped his control of the dragon, the flames melted the ice and fizzled out, the air dispersed, and the earth fell back to the ground albeit a little warm.

"Amelie, you're going to hurt yourself again." He said, smiling as he walked over to her. "I've already told you, I can't heal a headache yet."

"Why can't I do it." She snapped angrily at herself. She had been trying to get Aaron to hear her inside his mind, like he could hear Tala. "Talas told me how to do it. I don't understand why it won't work for me."

Aaron smiled softly at her. "I'm sure it will, but you can't force it. We've both told you, it was a complete accident." She shook her head, still angry at herself. "And one hell of a surprise, honestly it scared the crap out of me. I thought I was going mad." She let out a little laugh, then looked even angrier, almost as though she was mad at herself for finding it funny. "Imagine just going about your day and out of nowhere Tala's voice starts talking to you in your head." She laughed again. "What would you do if all of a sudden you could hear Ajit inside your head?"

Her small laugh died on her lips, she frowned and looked towards where Ajit and Tala were practicing their sphere shields. "To be honest, I'd just be happy he was talking to me again."

Aarons shoulders slumped. "He's still being weird around you then?" Ajit had not spoken to her since Aaron had proven that he could hear Tala speak inside his mind.

She shook her head, then shrugged. "He'd probably say something stupid anyway."

"Did you ever go bowling back on Earth?" Aaron asked her, an idea for a bit of fun suddenly hitting him.

"Where did that come from? That's a very random question." He just looked at her waiting for her to answer. "I did, a few times. I was never very good at it though."

"I bet you were never the ball though." He smiled at her as he built his sphere shield, lifting himself off the ground and nodding towards the other two.

Amelie looked from him to Tala and Ajit, the confused look melting from her face as she slowly realised what he meant. “Oh, that is brilliant.” She said and laughed properly.

Half an hour later, all four of them were laughing hysterically as Ajit laid on his back three feet above the ground and Aaron was upside down next to him. The two girls perfectly upright declaring themselves winners.

Aaron rolled his shield, so that he was upright again then lowered himself to the ground, Ajit on the other hand preferred to just cut his shield off and fall to the ground. Amelie was next to him quickly to help him up, instead he pulled her to the ground next to him and kissed her lightly. When they pulled apart, both of them looked happier than they had been in weeks.

Amelie looked at Aaron and he finally heard her voice break through into his mind. *‘Thank you.’*

After a moment of surprise, he smiled at her and replied. *‘You are very welcome.’*

Amelie looked extremely shocked at the same time a voice came from the door.

“Well, I must admit. That was rather impressive.” They all looked up to see Professor Flak standing in the doorway. “To be clear, I mean the game you were all playing. Not what happened after, I have no interest in the fraternising of my students. We are all adults, despite appearances.”

Aaron looked to Ajit and Amelie to see them both bright red and standing up quickly. “We were just having a little fun professor, blowing off a little steam.” He explained to her, unsure as to why he felt so nervous.

She shook her head. “I most vehemently disagree, Mr Scott. When you first produced a shield so perfect that it lifted you off the ground, I assumed it was an All-Power ability.” She looked to Amelie, Ajit, and Tala. “What I have just witnessed from the three of you, proves how wrong I was.” She shook her head. “I can honestly say that I have never been happier to be proven wrong.”
Her gaze moved to Aaron. “Excellent work in teaching your friends, Mr Scott.” She smiled, Aaron let out a relieved breath. “I am curious, do you think you would be able to teach me the same. When the new term begins of course.”

Aaron couldn’t help but laugh. “Yes professor. I would be very happy to.”

“Excellent.” She smiled again. “Excellent. Then I can teach the other Air professors. Then you four will have to think of a name and some rules for that game of yours. That looked highly amusing, not to mention an incredible way to test shield strength.” She laughed as she turned and started to walk away. “Blowing off steam indeed. The four of you may well have just invented the best Air mage sport that Nerium has ever seen.”

21

It was the last day of the Spring Celebration break and the four of them were sat by the tree, its branches now filled with lush green leaves, giving the group some shade as the weather continued to heat up. They were enjoying their last free day before the next term started when Heidi walked over to them.

“Hi, do you mind if I join you?” She asked, they nodded, and she sat with them. “We’ve just got back. I just wanted to talk to you quickly.” She said to Aaron.

“Ok, what’s wrong?” He asked her.

She looked uneasy for a moment. “Well, we went on the tour looking at different villages and towns. It’s not like I expected to be honest, but that’s not why I came over.” She tried to smile but it ended up looking like a grimace. “Everywhere we went, and almost everyone we spoke to.” She looked sadly at Aaron. “They all thought that the whole school should band together and, well, get rid of you.”

Aaron nodded. “Yeah, I met with the Prime Mage a while ago. I’m not surprised. But thank you for the warning, Heidi.” He smiled at her. “Why wasn’t it like you were expecting?”

"Yeah, I wanted to warn you. Most of us don't agree with them, of course. But there might be some." She nodded at him. "Maybe I'm just being naïve, but I was expecting everywhere to be, I don't know." She shook her head and looked at the ground. "Single branch mages don't like dual mages to live in the same town as them. It's like they're afraid that the dual mages will infect them with something. It's just." She let out a sigh. "Disappointing."

"Really?" Tala asked, obviously surprised. "What do they think will happen?"

Heidi continued talking to the group, but Aaron was distracted. He could feel anger radiating from the direction of the common room. He recognised the feeling, Dylan had changed his mind about attacking Aaron again. Aaron looked around his group and, as he felt Dylan's anger getting closer, he quickly made a decision. He quietly stood, claiming he was stretching his legs, and walked around to the other side of the tree. He saw Dylan and ten others walk out of the common room, he turned back to his group of friends.

"Sorry about this." He said to them as he lifted the earth like a blanket over them, to hide and protect them in a hollow mound of earth that none of Dylan's attacks could get through. Then he walked back towards Dylan. "Welcome back Dylan. Did you enjoy the tour?"

"Everyone out there agrees with me. You need to be stopped." He shouted, pointing at Aaron as his ten friends spread out next to him.

“I need to be stopped, do I? I haven’t done anything, Dylan.” Aaron tried to reason with him. “You are the one that keeps attacking me.”

Dylan didn’t answer him, he just shouted. “Do it now!” And every one of his friends attacked.

Aaron was obviously expecting this, and every attack hit his shield, instead of deflecting them he made all the attacks swirl around him. Dylan and his friends were unknowingly strengthening Aaron’s shield. As their attack spells blocked out the light, Aaron contemplated what he could do to stop this attack. Thankfully, his friends were safely hidden away so they could not be used to hurt Aaron. An idea came to him, and he smiled.

A few minutes earlier, in the main hall, Head Mistress Taylor was stood with the returning professors. The Prime Mage had returned with them, and he did not look happy.

“Head Mistress.” He began, barely hiding his frustration. “Would you care to tell me why I have not received a report on the All-Power for the last two weeks?”

“Prime Mage, how good to see you again.” She greeted him. “For the last two weeks, the school has been on the Spring Celebration break. Surely you don’t expect Mr Scott to be watched while there is no learning taking place.”

“That, Head Mistress is exactly what I expect. I want the All-Power observed every second possible.”

Since Mr Scott's arrival, Head Mistress Taylor had gotten used to constantly observing the vibrations in the air, vigilantly watching for any attacks. "Prime Mage, you must realise that." She stopped as she felt the beginnings of attacks on the grounds.

"Realise what, Head Mistress?" The Prime Mage impatiently asked her.

Head Mistress Taylor had turned toward the door. "Everybody, come with me." She ordered as she set off running, every professor followed without question. The Prime Mage a few steps behind them. Together they ran out of the courtyard and stopped when they saw what was unfolding.

In front of them they saw a group of students attacking a swirling mass of rocks, flames, roaring wind, and ice. With every attack they sent into the mass, the larger it got. As they watched, the swirling mass rose into the air and slowly formed into a gigantic dragon, with a body made of molten rock, eyes and spikes of ice, and electricity sparking out of its nose.

"It's the All-Power! Get him!" Shouted the Prime Mage.

Head Mistress Taylor effortlessly deflected the stream of fire that the Prime Mage had just unleashed towards the dragon.

"Prime Mage, compose yourself! You will not attack anyone on my school grounds." She shouted at him. "Take a moment to look at what is happening." She pointed to the attackers, not towards the dragon. The dragon was sat on its hind legs absorbing every attack sent into it. It made no move whatsoever to attack. All around it, the attackers were one by one stopping their attacks, holding their hands, palms together above their heads and lifting off the ground, as though they were being chained up.

"I, I don't understand. What's going on?" The Prime Mage asked.

As the last attacker was invisibly restrained, the dragon shook its head and started to talk.

Through the dragons' eyes, Aaron could see his attackers, looking so small. Like they should have always looked to him, like ants. He could crush them right now. He could use his dragon to chew them to pieces. Pathetic little creatures, they were so much less than he was. He should kill every single one of them. How dare they think that they even had the right to attack him?

Aaron realised what he was thinking and shook his head, the dragon shook its head along with him. Then he spoke to them, his voice booming out of the dragons' mouth.

"Dylan, please stop doing this." He said looking directly at Dylan through the dragons' eyes, Dylan looked terrified. "I am not what you think I am. I know you have all been taught that All-Powers are evil. But I am not."

"How can you say that?" Dylan screamed at him, it was the first time he had entered into a conversation with him. "You're a bloody dragon, of course you are."

Aaron walked out from behind the dragon. "No Dylan, I'm not." He replied, his voice still coming from the dragon. "This dragon is your attacks, all I did was control each element and form the dragon. And I only did that to distract you all, you were attacking your own attack spells. And while you did that, I used the air to restrain you all."

Aaron dropped his control of the dragon, and, like the smaller one he had made in the Air Fire Classroom, the fire melted the ice and fizzled out, the electricity turned to static in the air and red hot rocks fell to the ground.

"Again, Dylan, please stop doing this." He tried again. Then he saw a mass of professors walking around the restrained attackers with shocked looks on their faces.

Head Mistress Taylor instructed the other professors to take Aaron's attackers away and into detention, then she turned to Aaron. "How did they get you alone, Mr Scott?"

"Oh." Aaron shouted, suddenly remembering his friends. He turned and moved the mound of earth that they were hidden beneath.

"What the hell Aaron?" Ajit shouted.

"You have to let us help you." Amelie shot at him.

Tala and Heidi just stared at the eleven attackers being led away. “Are you OK?” They asked together. Tala turning angrily to Heidi.

“Oh please, he’s allowed other friends.” Heidi said to her.

“You’re all safe, that’s what matters.” Aaron smiled, thankful that they were all ok and turned back to Head Mistress Taylor. He was more than a little shocked to see the Prime Mage stood with her.

The Prime Mage looked at Aaron but spoke to the head mistress. “I will expect a report on Friday as usual.” He said as he walked away.

Aaron watched with Head Mistress Taylor as the Prime Mage left. “You manage to surprise everyone, with every attack, Mr Scott.” The head mistress said as she turned back to him. “What was that?”

“The dragon?” He asked, she nodded. “Well, I’ve been practicing controlling each element over the Spring Celebration break.” He said as he created small dragons just as he had in the Air Fire Classroom. “One day when I was practicing, I wondered if I could combine them.” He slowly combined the four small dragons to show her. “That’s what I did with all of their attacks.”

Head Mistress Taylor inspected the dragon floating in front of her. “That is exceptional work, Mr Scott. But this, is the size of a small dog. What I just saw was a dragon almost as tall as the school.” She shook her head. “Exceptional.” She looked toward his friends. “And what of your friends? How did they end up under the ground like that?”

“I could feel Dylan’s anger radiating from the common room, I knew that he was coming to attack me again.” He looked to his friends, but somehow, he did not notice that they were all silently seething. “I knew he would attack them to get to me. I wasn’t going to let him do that.”

“OK, I will have a follow up question from that.” Head Mistress Taylor began. “But first, you know I have to ask, was restraining them your first idea?”

“Of course, it was.” He lied. “I’ve told you before head mistress, I am not going to kill anyone.”

The head mistress nodded. “Ok, I had to ask, you know I did.” She looked to his friends. “Does anyone need a Healer?”

“No. We’re all fine. He trapped us underground.” Tala said staring at Aaron.

This time Aaron noticed the anger in her voice, confused he turned to look at her.

Head Mistress Taylor nodded and looked back to Aaron. “Now, what did you mean when you said that you could feel his anger?”

He looked at her, surprised that he had forgotten to mention it, after the last time he was attacked. “You know when you just have a feeling that something is wrong?” The professor nodded. “It’s like that but I can tell its anger, and not mine. I felt it last time he attacked but I guess I forgot to tell you about it. I, we, were all pretty shaken last time.” He looked to his friends. “This time I’ve had more training and, when they started to attack, I had the idea about the dragon.”

The professor nodded. “OK, we will talk further about that in our interview on Friday. For now, get some rest, all of you. Lessons begin again in the morning.” And she turned and walked away.

Aaron turned to Tala and the others. “You’re all safe, that’s why I did it.” None of them answered him. One by one, they turned and walked away from him, without saying a word, and made their way back to the common room. Tala leaving last. *‘Tala?’* Aaron thought into her mind.

‘Don’t.’ She shouted back into his. *‘Just don’t.’*

22

Aaron paced back and forth in his library. "I did the right thing." He said to the empty room. "They needed to be protected." He continued pacing. "They aren't as strong as I am." He said as he threw himself down onto his sofa. He needed to calm down.

This was the first time since they had started the Spring Celebration break that he was alone in his room, Tala had been in there with him for the whole break. He had not meditated for weeks, he settled on meditation to try and relax.

Twenty minutes later Aaron sat with his eyes closed, more worked up than when he had first walked back into his room. He had tried to meditate, but no matter how hard he tried, he could not bring his focus back to his breathing. His mind kept going back to the attack, in particular his thoughts about crushing his attackers, thoughts about how much less than him his attackers were. And thoughts of every other time he had had thoughts like that, like the two other times Dylan had tried to attack him. How he had thought of tearing his flesh open and frying him from the inside with bolts of electricity, how he had imagined burning the flesh off his skin.

But it had not been just Dylan that he had had these thoughts about, he had imagined tearing the Prime Mage limb from limb in their first meeting, imagined expanding an air bubble inside his head until it popped like a grape.

While he had been trying to meditate, those thoughts had been going round and round in his head like a gruesome slideshow. For some reason mixed in with those thoughts, was the last dream he had. The dream where he had spoken with Aban Fasil, where he had learnt that he could perform magic from his dreams while he was awake. The dream in the secret room somewhere in the school.

The secret room.

Aarons eyes shot open. He could not believe that he had not thought of it yet. He stood up, thought about walking into the room and instantly a green doorway opened up in front of him.

He stepped through.

The room was exactly as it had been in the dream, circular, no windows, eight paintings with the same smokeless torches that were in the rest of the school, they lit themselves as soon as he set foot in the room, and one door. He checked around the room, looking for anything that he may have missed in the dream. There was nothing else. He walked to the door to see where it went, he pushed it open, surprised by how heavy it felt. He stepped through and his anger and frustration from the events of the day switched to shock, he had just walked from a secret room through a secret door, into his own library. The door had been so heavy because it was one of his bookshelves, he stood in his library looking back into the secret room.

He stepped back into the room and walked around looking at the paintings, stopping in front of the painting of Isabella Lockton. “You built this place. What’s the purpose of this room?” He asked the painting.

Before he had been pulled to Nerium from Earth, Aaron had seen a lot of films where paintings talked back to you, he was not expecting that to happen, he was not expecting anything. He especially was not expecting what happened next.

Smoke poured from the painting, heavy smoke that sunk to the ground. The smoke flowed along the floor, it moved around Aaron and stopped in the centre of the room where it rose up to form the shape of a person. It coalesced and solidified into Isabella Lockton, or the ghost of her, Aaron noticed that the person in front of him was not completely solid, he could still see through her smoky body.

She looked at him for a moment then smiled. “It certainly took you long enough to get here.” She said, her voice gravelly and aged. “That useless Fasil showed you this room two weeks ago.” She said as she drifted to the painting of Aban Fasil. “To answer your question, this room is to allow All-Powers to speak with their predecessors. Somewhat annoyingly though, only two have found it before you.” She looked back to Aaron. “Surprisingly, the useless Fasil was the first.”

“I’ll guess that Anastasia was the second.” Aaron overcame his shock at her sudden appearance. The ghostly Isabella shook her head. “Henry Carmine?” She shook her head again. “Alexander Miller then? As all he wanted was to isolate himself from this world, I’m surprised you’d want to talk to him.” He noticed she was still shaking her head. Aaron stared at her, his brows furrowed. Then he remembered the painting of the silhouette from his dream, his eyes moved to it and back to Isabella, she was smiling this time. He moved to the painting of the dark form. “Who are you?”

Just like it had done with Isabella Lockton, smoke poured from the painting and solidified into the form of a person. Only this time it stayed looking like black smoke. “I’m not sure if I can trust you yet.” The smoky form said in a whispery tone, its voice sounding like a jumble of many voices, giving no clue as to the gender of the mysterious All-Power.

Aaron looked to Isabella, she was just smiling at him. “OK, if you’re not ready to tell me who you are yet.” He began. “Maybe you could tell me why no one knows about you?”

The smoky form nodded slowly. “That, I can do.” It set off gliding around the room, taking its time to look at each of the paintings as it went.

“When I arrived here on Nerium, time was frozen.” It began to explain as it got back to its own painting, it ran a smoky hand over the frame and continued. “There was a being there waiting for me. A being that only I and the great Isabella Lockton have known.” It looked to Isabella and bowed its smoky head to her. Isabella only smiled back at it. “This being told me everything I needed to know. They instructed me not to reveal myself as an All-Power. That I was to masquerade as a dual mage, and they gave me a mission.” It turned its smoky head back to Aaron. “I did what they said and completed my mission. It took me thirty five years to complete it, but I completed my mission.” Its smoky form glided around Aaron. “And it can never be undone.” It whispered into his ears as it went round him. Then the smoke shot back into its painting, and the smoky form was gone.

Aaron turned back to Isabella to see her staring at the painting of Nicholas Garnier. He walked over to stand next to her. “He did not deserve what they did to him.” She said without looking at Aaron. “He had so much potential, he and I met many times while he meditated. I knew his mind better than any All-Power that has come after him.” She turned to Aaron. “Those pathetic pretenders kicked him to death like he was a dog.”

“Pretenders?” Aaron asked.

“Pretenders to power, they think that because they elect someone, that that someone has the power to do what is necessary. They don’t, they are all weak.” She spat suddenly angry. “You know. I know you do. I know you have felt the anger of your predecessors.”

“I have.” He admitted. “And I know that, given time, I could be stronger than any of them.” He said looking around the room at all the All-Powers that came before him, he turned back to look her in her smoky eyes. “But that doesn’t mean I have to kill people. Just because I can.”

She looked disappointed. “Then you will be just as useless as Fasil.” She glided over to look at Aban Fasil’s painting. “He was weak too. Constantly moaning ‘We are no better than our fellow mages’ he used to whine at me when he came here.”

“But we are better than them.” Aaron said, shocking Isabella enough for her to turn back and look at him again. “Better in the sense that we can do more magic than they can, but killing for the sake of killing just makes us murderers.” She looked away again shaking her head. “There are men on Earth that speak of peace and harmony, they have followers in the millions. Followers that hang on their every word.” She looked back at him, suddenly curious. “Then there are dictators that kill their own people to show power. Every time they are brought down by their own people, that is what has happened to every All-Power. All of you killed because you could, or you tried to rule through fear and intimidation.” Isabella began to glide around the room again. “Did any of you question this, or has every All-Power that came before me been a psycho killer just waiting for an excuse?”

Isabella’s smoky form shot to Aaron, stopping inches from his face. “We killed because those pathetic lesser mages need to be put in their place.”

"Really?" Aaron asked, not intimidated by her ghostly form. "Then explain Anastasia, she killed for fun. She enjoyed it, laughed about it."

Her smoky form moved to Anastasia's painting. "She." Isabella tilted her smoky head. "Was special. Her mind was warped before she got to Nerium." She moved back to Aaron. "You have potential, Aaron Scott, you may return to this room to speak with us again. Do not bring any other mage into this sanctuary, not even another All-Power, should one arrive. They must find this place on their own." With that, her smoky form began to return to its frame.

"I have one more question, if I may?" Aaron asked before she had completely returned to her frame. She stopped and nodded, only her torso was left outside the painting. "Where is this room?"

"This is one of the rooms within Lock Tower. I created places just for All-Powers in the tower when I built this school. None have found any of the others." She said simply and she continued returning to her frame until Aaron was alone.

23

The next morning Aaron walked out of his room, a little saddened that his friends were not there waiting to walk to breakfast with him.

'Tala?' He sent sheepishly into her mind, hoping she would reply. He waited, but no answer came. Head down he started walking.

'We're in the main hall.' Tala's voice finally answered inside his head.

Aaron let out a sigh of relief and smiled as he was walking. *'Are you all still mad at me?'*

'Yes'. She answered plainly. *'But come and have breakfast anyway'*.

Aaron collected his breakfast and then found the table where Tala, Ajit and Amelie were all sat, he joined them, none of them looked up as he did. "I needed to protect you, you have to know that." He pleaded with them.

"No." Amelie said, finally looking up at Aaron. "No Aaron, you didn't. We aren't pets of yours that you need to protect." The force of her gaze made Aaron want to look away. "We aren't angry that you hid us underground."

“I am.” Ajit interrupted. “It was pitch black, we had no way out. If they had got the better of you.” He looked up at Aaron. “No one would have known we were there. No one would have come for us.”

Aaron had not thought of that, but he didn’t respond.

“We’re mad because you’d rather face these attacks alone than let us help.” Tala joined in but she didn’t look up.

“It’s not that.” Aaron started but he didn’t know why he had decided to hide them.

“You were in the Army, Aaron. You should know that a team is stronger together.” Amelie said.

Aaron also knew that a team was only as strong as its weakest link, that if a team did not work well together it would not work at all. But he chose not to say anything.

“And you trapped us in there with Heidi. You have no idea how whiny she is in the dark.” Tala added, almost laughing. She finally looked up at him. “Just don’t do something stupid like that again.” He looked into her eyes and immediately regretted his decision, he nodded. “We could hear everything in there. We heard you talk to Dylan, we heard him tell everyone to attack you. Then this weird rumbling noise, then your voice really loud. Talking about a dragon.” She shook her head. “We didn’t know what was happening.”

Aaron nodded and told them everything that had happened after he had hidden them. “Look, maybe I made the wrong decision in hiding you.”

"Maybe?" The three of them asked together.

"Ok, ok." Aaron responded with his hands raised. "I was wrong, I'm sorry. I made the wrong choice. I won't do it again." The three of them looked slightly less angry. "But, you might be about to get even madder at me." He went on to tell them everything that happened after they had all left the night before.

"Can we see it?" Ajit asked once Aaron had finished telling them about the room.

Aaron shook his head. "They'll never let me back in there if I do that."

Amelie looked unconvinced. "Why would you even want to go back there?" She asked.

"I know they're all nutters." He admitted. "But, I could learn a lot from them."

"It's not just that." Tala joined in. "You need to go back there." She looked at Aaron. "There's a secret All-Power? You need to find out who it is."

"And what was their mission?" Ajit added. "Oh, and she said it was one of the rooms in Lock Tower. One of them? How many more rooms are in there?"

Amelie shook her head. "I don't think those questions are worth risking talking to them though."

“What about the ‘being’ they talked about though?” Aaron asked her. She just shrugged. “I’m sorry Amelie, there are just too many questions to ignore that room.” She looked unconvinced. “How about this, I will only go to the room during the end of season breaks, and only once each break. Does that sound ok?”

“I’m outnumbered, I guess that’s the best I’m going to get.” She said defeatedly. “Just, think carefully about what you ask them. And don’t let them seduce you into being an abuser.”

Aaron nodded, slightly curious about her choice of words, she could have said murderer or villain or even bad guy. But she said abuser. He decided not to question it then, it looked like she wasn’t in any mood for conversation.

Every one of Aarons lessons went the same way, they all checked his control of the individual elements. Every one of them moved him on to something different.

Professor Flak moved on to flight. “There are two main ways of achieving flight.” She said after she had assessed his element control. “The most difficult but safest way to fly is to control the air around you and use it to carry you through the air.” She demonstrated by flying a lap around the classroom. “The second, and much less controllable. Is to whip the air around you into a wind strong enough to lift you off the ground.” She once again flew a lap around the classroom, this time looking far less graceful.

"Water breathing is an incredibly useful skill." Professor Loam had said. "Admittedly not an everyday skill, but in case you suddenly find yourself underwater. Or in most cases, it is used for fishing." She noticed Aarons confused look and smiled. "Not all food on Nerium is gruel, Mr Scott." She then went on to tell him how Water mages could form an air bubble around their heads and constantly fill it with oxygen pulled from the water, therefore giving them the ability to remain underwater indefinitely.

"Now, Mr Scott." Professor Turner said as he started pacing round the room. "The Earth Air duality is an incredibly useful combination." He turned to look at Aaron. "Of course, every professor will say that about their own speciality. But." He resumed his pacing. "For example. This very school was built using Earth and Air magic, not Fire and not Water." Again, he looked back at Aaron. "Yes, it was built by an All-Power. But she used Earth and Air magics to build it." He began with showing Aaron how to use Earth magic to grow a pillar of earth.

"This is a little pointless, let's be honest." Professor Stein said on Wednesday morning as he checked Aaron's control of fire. "But we have to check. We all saw that dragon of yours." He smiled at Aaron. "It truly was magnificent Mr Scott. The way you strengthened the ice so that it wouldn't melt inside the flaming rock." He shook his head in admiration. "Magnificent." He smiled at Aaron again. "What we will be moving onto is extinguishing of fires. Surprisingly it is much easier to create fire than it is to put one out."

"The first thing I would like to ask you about." Head Mistress Taylor said in her interview with Aaron that Friday. "Is your ability to sense feelings."

Aaron shook his head. "I can't sense feelings, professor. Just Dylan's anger when he's about to attack." He looked out of the window, he liked the view from the head mistress's office. "I can't tell when people are happy or worried or anything like that."

"Yet it is still not something I have heard of before." The head mistress interjected.

"I think I've read about it." Aaron added. "I have a book called *Notable All-Power abilities uncommon in other Mages*. Have you heard of it?"

"That All-Power book I have heard of, yes." She said as she stood and walked to the bookcase behind her desk. She picked a book from the shelf and walked back to her seat handing the book to Aaron.

"It was one of the first books I read in my self-study sessions." He said as he flicked through the pages. "It's one of the smaller books." He added a little guiltily. The head mistress just smiled at him. "Here it is,

It was noted that Henry Carmine had the ability to sense attacks from other mages before any spell had been cast. It is unclear how he was able to do this or whether it is an ability that can be learnt by other mages

.

This ability was noted both during his time at Doctrina and in the years after his tenure as Prime Mage."

Aaron looked from the book to the head mistress. "That's what I think it is."

For weeks Aaron struggled in each of his lessons, this proved to massively frustrate him. He had gotten used to magic coming to him easily and now that it wasn't, he wanted to know why. What had changed?

"Maybe nothing's changed." Amelie said one weekend while the four of them were practicing. She was trying to create a small tornado in the palm of her hand. "Think about it, think about what you've already learnt. It's all the same."
"What do you mean? I've learnt loads of different stuff." Aaron asked as he struggled to hover six feet above the ground.

Amelie smiled as she managed to hold the tornado steady. "Yes. But, they were all the same." Aaron crashed to the ground and her tornado faded away while she tried not to laugh at him. "All shields, all deflection, all control. Now you're learning something different in all of your classes."

Aaron considered this as he stood up and brushed himself off.

"And, don't forget the fact that you're probably still thinking about your secret room." Tala joined in as she held a small tornado in each hand. Aaron noticed Amelie shake her head, she still got annoyed whenever any of them mentioned the secret room.

"Or." Ajit jumped into the conversation. "Maybe you're letting the rest of us catch up." He said without lifting his head from the ground.

"Seeing as you never practice. I'd have to unlearn most of what I know to do that." Aaron laughed at him.

Ajit threw his hands out. "It's the weekend. Chill out."

"Do you practice on weekdays?" Tala asked.

"No, that's what class time is for." He laughed back at her.

Aaron concentrated on the air underneath Ajit and whipped it up into a small tornado, lifting Ajit a few feet off the ground.

"Argh! Stop it. What are you doing?" Ajit shouted as he flailed around above the tornado.

"Control the air." Aaron shouted back. "Stop me yourself."

"Just put me down, I'll practice. I promise." Ajit pleaded.

Aaron shook his head. "No. Control the air, or next time Dylan and his goons attack me, I'll have to hide you on your own." Ajit grunted as he tried to slow the air underneath him, Aaron felt the air slow, and he smiled. "Yes, that's it, keep going." The air continued to slow, and Ajit slowly lowered to the ground.

Ajit stood up scowling at Aaron. "That wasn't funny."

"Showed you that you could do it when you actually try though didn't it." Aaron said.

"And it was a bit funny." Amelie laughed.

Later that evening, Aaron had just said goodnight to Tala and gone back to his room, he was just about ready to get into bed when there was a knock on his door. He went to see who it was and found Tala looking slightly traumatised.

"Can I sleep here?" She asked, barely more than a whisper.

He invited her in. "Of course, what's wrong?"

"I." She shook her head. "I just walked in on Amelie and Ajit."

"Oh." He laughed loudly.

"It's not funny, I can never unsee that now." She said, still shaking her head, as though she was trying to shake the memory out of her mind.

"Did they see you?"

"No, they were." She looked at him, still looking traumatised. "Busy."

Aaron laughed loudly again. "Why didn't they go to Ajit's room?"

“I don’t know, I didn’t hang around to ask.” She rolled her eyes at him. “I need a bath.”

While she was in the bathroom Aaron got into bed, he laid there waiting for Tala to wash the memory off of her, still chuckling to himself. Then he heard something that really was not meant for him. When Tala came out of the bathroom, he was not laughing anymore.

“Amelie.” Aaron said nervously, the next morning as the four of them were walking to the tree. “Can we have a word?” Tala and Ajit looked confused. “About the room, nothing important.” He lied to them. He and Amelie wandered away from the other two. “Ok, just act normal. Because you know those two are watching us.” He said as they walked. “Could you do me a favour?”

“That depends on what it is.” She laughed.

He tried to smile at her. “The next time you and Ajit are.” He paused, trying to find the right word. “Together.” He settled on. “Please, please, please. Keep me as far from your mind as possible.”

“I don’t understand.” She said, looking genuinely confused.

“Last night.” He stopped again, trying to find the right words. “At your, shall we say, your peak. I heard you, in my head.”

Her eyes widened as she realised what he was talking about. “Oh god!”

Aaron nodded. “Yep, that was it. Just a lot less horrified.”

“Oh god!” She repeated.

Aaron held up a hand. “Please stop. I heard that enough last night.”

“I’m so sorry, I was thinking that I had to thank you for getting us together. Then I.”

“La la la la la la.” Aaron sang as he plugged his ears with his fingers. “I don’t need to hear any more details.” He interrupted her. “Just think about something, anything else.” He smiled at her. “Come on, lets get back to those two. We’ll tell them I was asking you for your honest opinion on what I should ask the paintings.”

‘What was that really about?’ Tala asked inside his mind after they had given their fake explanation to her and Ajit.

Aaron sat next to her. *‘Well, you saw them last night, I heard them.’* He heard her stifle a laugh. *‘Apparently, she was thinking about thanking me for getting them together when, things got to their best. I heard what came after.’* This time she couldn’t hide her laugh.

“I wish you two would talk out loud.” Ajit said shaking his head.

Amelie just sat looking at the ground. “Can you just, not talk about it?”

Ajit looked between the three of them. “Talk about what?”

“I’m sorry.” Tala laughed. “I saw it and I was mortified, but he got the soundtrack.” She said laughing even harder.

“Saw what?” Ajit asked, looking very confused. “What soundtrack?”

Amelie put her head in her hands.

“What do you think I could have walked in on last night?” Tala asked Ajit.

Ajit suddenly figured out what they were talking about. “Oh god!” he said, his eyes opening wide.

“Don’t say that!” Aaron said loudly to him.

Amelie screamed into her hands and Tala laughed even harder.

24

The months that followed passed in a blur, Tala spent almost every night with Aaron as Ajit was in her room with Amelie. As a result, all four of them grew closer. The two couples were closer, Tala had gotten so used to walking in on Amelie and Ajit that it no longer mortified her, she just shielded her eyes, got what she needed from her room and went straight back to Aarons room.

At least once a week Amelie would cling to Aaron's arm and thank him for getting Ajit to admit his feelings. There was also a noticeable change in her behaviour, Aaron had noticed. She walked less rigidly, she wasn't looking over her shoulder as much and she was much, much happier.

Ajit had finally started to practice with the other three and was making a lot of progress, almost to the point where he was catching up with Tala and Amelie.

Aaron, on the other hand was still frustrated by the lack of his own progress. He had managed to fly sufficiently enough to move on to something new. Professor Flak was now teaching him how to use the air to carry his voice the way Professor Horton did in their first lessons, it had been Aaron's suggestion.

"This was perfected by Prime Mage Proctor when she was a professor here, she taught Professor Horton. Before she was Prime Mage of course." Professor Flak had said. "Sounds, as I am sure you know are vibrations in the air. Once you are able to isolate the vibrations created by your own voice we can go further with projection."
He was still struggling with underwater breathing, he had managed to create the bubble he needed but was still unable to pull oxygen from the water to refill it. He had been making some progress with growing pillars but not enough to move on.

Once he had finally got the hang of extinguishing fires, Professor Stein had moved him onto something he said might be useful. "As autumn is fast approaching, you may find use for this." He smiled at Aaron. "Given how you and your friends enjoy the solitude and shade of the tree outside the courtyard." He went on to show Aaron how to heat the air around him. "When you master that, I will show you how to heat the outer edge whilst simultaneously evaporating falling rain drops. Thereby keeping you, and your friends warm and dry. This is something only Water Fire mages can do." He tilted his head. "Water mages can divert raindrops away from themselves, and Fire mages can heat the air around them. But that only serves to warm the rain up." He added dismissively.

Aaron had managed to teach Professor Flak how to create a sphere shield. "You and your friends must still think of a name and rules for your game." She had said once she had finally managed it, it had taken her almost two months to perfect it, but she could now perform it well enough that she was now teaching the other Air professors. Aaron saw this as further proof that his dreams were not prophecy, he had now taught four dual mages instead of the two that his dream claimed.

Dylan and his friends had shown no remorse in their actions, in fact their resolve had hardened since their tour of Nerium. The professors had decided that they were a danger to the other students, and that they should remain in detention. They were escorted from the detention room for their lessons, then escorted back to the darkened room at the end of learning each day.

"The Prime Mage is showing, the tiniest signs of happiness with your reports." Head Mistress Taylor said to Aaron in his weekly interview the Friday before the start of the Summer Celebration break. "I think it is because you are struggling in some of your classes."

Aaron shifted in his seat. "At least someone's happy about it." He said glumly.

"Is that a sore subject?"

He nodded. "It's just, when I got here everything came so easily." He sighed and looked out of the window. "It's a little annoying that I haven't picked them up yet."

The head mistress nodded thoughtfully. "When you first arrived, your initial progress, was beyond what anyone thought possible." She began. "With complete honesty. It scared a lot of people." Looking Aaron in the eye she smiled tightly. "Myself included." Letting out a sigh, she continued. "Now that you are struggling in some areas. Albeit showing more progress than other mages. It shows that you are not an all-powerful unstoppable mage, at least not yet anyway." The head mistress stood and walked to a table by the wall to pour herself a drink. "People are still scared of what you could be capable of. I am not, but I have gotten to know you. The people outside of these grounds only know what the Prime Mage tells them of you. And, as he is afraid of you, of what you may become, whether he intends to or not, he is passing that fear to the rest of Nerium." She walked back and sat down behind her desk, taking a drink as she went. "The simple fact that not every magic comes naturally to you is alleviating some fears." She looked questioningly at Aaron. "Do you understand this?"

"I do." He nodded. "It's still annoying to me though."

She smiled at him. "I am sure it is." Her smile vanished. "Onto the subject of Mr Lawson." She sighed. "He will be leaving the grounds with the rest of the third years. For their second and final tour of Nerium."

"Should I be ready for another attack, when they get back?" He asked her.

She shook her head. "Mr Lawson and his friends will have extra professors observing them throughout their tour. And will be escorted back to the detention room upon their return." She watched him as he let out a breath and relaxed his shoulders. "However, this does not mean that he won't convince others to make an attempt. I think it unlikely, but something you should bear in mind."

That evening, after the third and fourth year students had left for the Summer Celebrations break. Aaron, Tala, and Amelie were sat at the tree watching Ajit practice flying. The three dual mages had moved onto flying that day, it was the first thing that Ajit was interested in practicing. Amelie laid her head on Aaron's shoulder as she watched Ajit hover unsteadily a foot above the ground. "Thank you, Aaron."

"You have to stop saying that." He smiled at her. "You two would've got together at some point."

"Yeah, but who knows how long that would've taken." She said, still with her head on his shoulder. Ajit fell to the ground and swore loudly. "He's an idiot." She laughed. "But I'm happier than I have been in years. Before we got here I." She stopped. "He makes me happy."

"Are you ever going to tell us about your life on Earth?" Tala asked looking up at her, she was laid resting her head on Aarons legs.

"It doesn't matter anymore." She answered shaking her head. "We're never going back there." She said, a smile spreading across her face.

Ajit walked to them, exhausted from the effort of trying to fly. “Hey Aaron, can we try that bath of yours that Tala won’t shut up about?” He asked pointing between himself and Amelie.

Aaron looked between the two of them. “Separately, yes. Together? Absolutely not.”

“Come on! Like you two haven’t.” He said throwing his hands into the air.

“Firstly - That, is none of your business.” Aaron laughed at him. “And secondly - Would you clean it after?”

“It’s a bath, you let the water out and it’s clean.” Ajit laughed.

“Ewww.” Tala groaned.

Aaron leaned his head down to Amelie’s ear. “Are you sure you’re happy?” He whispered to her. She just laughed. He stood up, eliciting complaints from the two girls.

“I was comfy then.” Tala complained as her head fell to the ground. Amelie shuffled over so Tala could rest her head on her legs.

“Sorry.” Aaron said back to them, then he looked to Ajit. “If you can catch me, then I might consider it.” He said to him as he started to feel the air press against him, and the ground begin to fall away from beneath his feet.

Ajit looked up, watching Aaron rise higher and higher. "Nobody likes a show off, Aaron." He said shaking his head.

Aaron hovered level with the top of the tree, he looked over the school, taking in for the first time just how imposing the building was. A great three-story slab of black stone, with a single tall tower rising from its centre, the tower that he now knew contained at least one secret room, solely for All-Powers. It looked from here to have a flat roof, the top floor being open to the sky. Next to it, the huge single story accommodation wing, which did have a flat roof. Aaron could see the entrance door and had a sudden thought, while he was thinking he heard Tala's voice.

"Don't go too high, Professor Flak said not to go too high."

Aaron lowered himself to the ground again. "Have you ever noticed that the walls to the accommodation wing are flat?" He asked the three of them.

"Walls normally are mate." Ajit said unhelpfully.

Aaron realised how ridiculous his question was. "Fair point." He admitted. "But what I mean is. The door into the common room is in the corner, yeah?" They nodded. "And the doors to our rooms are on the wall on the left as we go in, yeah?" They nodded again. "So where are they?" He asked pointing at the common room. The three of them looked in the direction he was pointing.

“Huh.” Amelie finally said, standing up.

Tala’s head hit the ground again. “Oh, come on. I just want to be comfortable.” She complained again.

Ajit sat next to her so she could use his leg as a pillow. “I’m not interested in another weird thing about this place.”

“Well, I am.” Amelie said to him as she started walking towards the common room with Aaron. “Don’t have too much fun.” She shouted back at them. “Should I be worried that I’m leaving my boyfriend with another girls head in his lap?” She asked Aaron.

He laughed. “Should my girlfriend have been worried when I had another girl resting her head on my shoulder?” He teased her. “They don’t see each other like that. I think we’re safe.” He smiled.

They reached the common room and opened the door, the eight doors leading to their rooms were right there on the wall to the left of the entrance. They closed the door again and walked to the left to see the flat wall going all the way to the end of the common room. They went back to the entrance door, opened it again and looked to the right, there was the one door into the fourth year dual rooms, they kept the door open and moved in and out of the door. The door to the fourth-year corridor on the inside and outside – nothing.

“Some of you finally noticed.” Came a bubbly high pitched voice.

They turned to see a second year they recognised but had never spoken to, walking towards them from the direction of the courtyard.

“I’m Rebecca, Air Fire dual mage. Second year.” She introduced herself with a big smile on her face. “I asked the professors about it last year, apparently not everyone notices it.” She began as she gestured to the walls of the common room. “I don’t see how they don’t see it really. There was this artist movement back on Earth in the 1950s and 60s where artists made buildings with pillars in the wrong places, or had like these stairs that were all actually just one floor, there were like people going up and down them but the stairs didn’t go anywhere except back to the beginning of the stairs. You know.”

She said all this while waving her hands around. Aaron and Amelie stood silently staring at her as she went on.

“Sorry, I tend to ramble.” She giggled. “Anyway, I only bring it up because those artworks made a lot of people think. You see, they were a lot for the eyes and the brain to accept. You know, you see it and you know it’s not possible but its right there in front of you.” She looked excitedly at the two first years, they were still just staring at her. “Our rooms are inside the walls, crazy right.” She smiled and walked past them into the common room.

Aaron and Amelie stared as she walked away. “I was in the Army for twenty four years, is that how normal people talk?” Aaron asked.

Amelie shrugged. “Don’t ask me, I was.” She stopped herself and shook her head. “She must have been American.” They looked at each other and burst into laughter as they set off back to the tree.

“The rooms are in the walls.” Aaron said. Once he had composed himself and as they walked. “I suppose we’ve seen weirder here.”

“I think we should probably just forget whatever was normal before we got here.” Amelie added as they got to the tree.

“Shhh.” Ajit said with a finger to his lips. “She’s asleep. Guess my legs are comfier than yours.” He smiled at them both.

Amelie looked at Aaron. “You’re not getting any sleep tonight.” She said with a chuckle.

“Well, now that she can’t remind me that Professor Flak said not to go too high, I’m going to see how high I can go.” Aaron said smiling.

“Well, she did say not to go too high.” Amelie said grabbing his arm.

“Come on, what’s going to happen? I can fly. I’m not going to fall.” He said cockily and took off. He rose higher and higher. The sounds of the ground fading behind him.

Aaron felt like he was leaving his worries behind, his worries about being an All-Power, his worries of when Dylan was next going to attack, or if someone else was going to try, his worries about his dreams.

Even the worries he didn't want to admit to himself, his worries about the dark thoughts he had been having since he had arrived on Nerium, worries that the painting of Isabella Lockton had pointed out to him. "I know you have felt the anger of your predecessors." She had said to him. She was right, he had. He had felt their rage build within him since he had got to this planet, since he had first found out that he was an All-Power. He had felt anger like he never had before.

But he was leaving all of that on the ground beneath him, up there in the air he was enjoying the silence, enjoying the fact that not even gravity could restrain him. He rose higher and higher still, he looked down to see the massive imposing school getting smaller and smaller, he held out a hand to see that his palm covered the whole school including the accommodation wing. He laughed enjoying the freedom.

Then his head hit something solid, his vision exploded into stars, momentum carried his body up and it crumpled against the solid something. The cushion of air that was holding him disappeared and he felt something warm run down the side of his face. Then everything went black.

Tala woke up as her head hit the ground, again. “Can none of you sit still?” Ajit had just stood up and he had walked over to where Amelie was standing. They were both looking up at the sky. She looked up to see what they were looking at, there was a dark speck in the sky. “What’s that?” She asked them. Neither of them answered. She looked up again, the speck was getting bigger. She looked carefully and noticed that it was a person. A person falling out of the sky. “Who is that?” She grabbed Ajit. “Who is that? Tell me that is not Aaron!” He looked at her and she could tell by the look on his face, she knew exactly who was falling through the sky. She looked up again and a scream poured from her mouth as though it had a life of its own.

Somewhere very far away Aaron heard screaming, he wanted to stay sleeping but he was cold. It was very windy in his room, why was it windy? He didn’t even have a window in his room. He tried to pull the covers over him, but he couldn’t feel his bed. The far away screaming was getting louder.

Suddenly he heard Isabella Lockton’s voice screaming inside his tired head. “Wake up you moron!”

He opened his eyes to see something flashing, light and dark, dark and light, light and dark. He closed his eyes and shook his head trying to wake up. He opened them again, it wasn’t flashing – he was rolling, rolling through the air.

It was the ground and the sky passing by his eyes so fast it looked like flashing as he fell from the sky, plummeting fast to the very solid ground of Nerium. Suddenly he remembered what was happening, the freedom and exhilaration of flying, then the pain of crashing into something he couldn't see high above the ground.

He was falling right now, falling to his death. Panic filled him and threatened to overwhelm him. The school was getting bigger, he had to fly, he tried to control the air around him, but he couldn't, the pain in his head stopping his concentration and the air was rushing by too fast for him to do anything.

He was going to die, he had to stop panicking. He tried to use the rushing air and turn it into wind to carry him to safety or at least slow his fall. He couldn't do it, he was going to die. He could make out the windows on the school as the ground flashed by.

He wasn't going to make it. The ground was coming too fast. He managed to put up his air shield just as the ground reached up to catch him. He heard his shield hit and dig into the ground, even inside his shield he heard bones break, felt searing pain all over his body and everything went black again.

Head Mistress Taylor was in her office, enjoying the start of the Summer Celebration. The third and fourth years had safely left the school grounds with their professors. She had had no shortage of volunteers for extra professors to watch Mr Lawson and his ilk, everyone was always happy to leave the school grounds.

She had just sat in her favourite armchair with a good book, when she heard a scream from outside. She had not felt any vibrations on the air to warn her that an attack was taking place, she jumped to the window. Just in time to see something dark streak past, so swiftly that she could not tell what it was. It hit with a loud boom, and it buried itself deep in the ground.

Then three people ran toward it from the tree, the tree where Mr Scott and his friends went to relax. Three people were running. She looked closer, it was Mr Scott's three friends, and the screams were coming from them. She suddenly had a horrible sinking feeling that she already knew what the something dark that had just dug itself into the ground was.

She set off running.

25

The darkness that had hold of Aaron battled with brightness that was too much for him to bear. He wanted the darkness to keep him, it was quiet in the dark, the brightness came with noises and visions that Aaron did not understand.

Things that did not make sense.

Tala shouting at someone. “I am not leaving.”

He had a strange feeling, as though things were moving inside his body.

Professor Iaso whispering. “No one move.”

An image of someone with a knife. Crashing noises.

Ajit yelling. “Just get her.”

Head Mistress Taylor shouting. “What on Nerium has got into you.”

Things that did not make sense.

Aaron opened his eyes and winced, he immediately felt a pain in his head, as though his skull had shrunk and was crushing his brain.

"You're awake! Please stay awake this time." Tala's voice came from next to him, she sounded tired.

"Why are you shouting?" He tried to whisper, but even his own voice sounded like he was screaming as loud as he could. He gingerly turned his head to look at her. "Where are we?"

"In Professor Iaso's healing classroom, your healing classroom." She looked tired, she looked like she had not slept in days. "Don't you recognise it?"

"Everything's blurry." He tried to reach a hand out to her but felt a blazing pain shoot up his arm. "How long have you been sat there?"

She smiled and gently laid her hand on his forehead. "Four days. You better hurry up and get better so I can beat the crap out of you."

He laughed and then suddenly stopped as he felt pain all over his body. "Four days! How bad was I hurt?"

Tala shook her head, tears starting to roll down her face. "It would only have been a few hours. But none of the healers could get their magic to you." She looked over Aaron to someone on the other side of him.

He turned his head to the other side and saw Head Mistress Taylor and Professor Iaso stood a few feet away.

"Just before you hit the ground." The Head Mistress began. "You managed to get your air shield up, I saw it from my office." She reached out a hand, Aaron saw it press against an invisible barrier. "Your shield is still up, Mr Scott. Even while you were unconscious, and gravely injured, your shield is so strong that no one could get through to help you." She looked from him to Tala. "The only person that could get close to you, the only person that could touch you. Was Miss Ramos here." She looked back to Aaron. "Over the last four days, we have been waiting and hoping that you would be able to heal yourself." She looked to her side, to Professor Iaso. "Now that you are awake. If you wouldn't mind lowering your shield so that Professor Iaso can heal you fully?"

Aaron felt the air around him to find that she was telling him the truth, his air shield was definitely up. He slowly lowered it, it took a lot longer than it normally would have. The concentration caused his head to feel as though it was splitting open. As the shield lowered, Aaron felt himself lower and gently lay on a bed that had been placed underneath him. "It's down." He whispered finally.

Professor Iaso stepped forward and held her hands out over him, palms facing towards him. "You have managed to heal your head injury enough to regain consciousness." The professor began as she scanned his broken body with her magic. "And you have thankfully healed significant internal bleeding. Incredible work Mr Scott." She smiled down at him. "But you still have a broken arm, both legs are broken, and you have several broken ribs. You are in for a few unpleasant hours."

She began with his head, easing and removing the brain crushing pain he was feeling. Aaron thought that felt extremely pleasant. But then she moved on to his bones and for the next few hours he felt white hot pain as the professor fused his bones back together. By the time she had finished with his bones, the pain in his head was back. It took her less than five minutes to heal his headache and Aaron was up and walking around again.

“Good as new.” He said as he walked around the classroom. “Thank you, Professor.” Professor Iaso smiled at him.

“Good.” Head Mistress Taylor said, but she did not sound happy. “Now, perhaps you would like to explain exactly what you were thinking.”

“I was flying, and the higher I got the less worried I felt.” He began. “It was so quiet up there, I didn’t have to think about how the whole world was against me. Or who was going to try to kill me next.” He smiled at the feeling of freedom he had felt. “I kept going higher and higher. It was, nice.” Then he reached a hand up and ran it across the back of his head. “Then I crashed into something, and everything went dark.”

Head Mistress Taylor shook her head. “That, Mr Scott. Would be the boundary of the school grounds.” She shook her head again. “It is almost six thousand feet high.”

“I did warn you not to go too high, Professor Flak warned you not to go too high.” Tala said, punching him in his newly healed arm.

Aaron shook his head. "Why is there a boundary all the way up there?" He asked the head mistress.

"What did you think marked the end of the school grounds?" The head mistress answered his question with one of her own.

"Oh, I don't know. A fence!" He said throwing his arms into the air. "Do you mean that we are trapped under an invisible dome?"

"Not trapped under, Mr Scott." She shook her head. "Protected by. We are not the only inhabitants of this world."

Aaron and Tala looked at each other. "Other inhabitants that we need to be protected from?" Tala asked the head mistress.

"No, Miss Ramos." She shook her head. "There has never been a major battle between the races. But the precaution of the barrier was put in place centuries ago, every Air mage that has taught in this school since its creation has strengthened it. It is currently estimated to be around thirty feet thick. It stretches out ten miles in each direction from the school and, like I said, almost six thousand feet high."

"Why have we not learnt about these other 'races' that we need protecting from? Why is that not the first thing we are taught here?" Aaron asked.

"Just the one other race and we do not need protecting from them, the barrier is simply a precaution. And, as students do not leave the school grounds until their third year, there is no need to teach you about them until your second year." She began. "You will be in your second year soon enough. You will learn about them then."

"But." Aaron began to question her, but she cut him off.

"No! You will learn about them soon enough." She ended the line of questioning. "The barrier also serves to protect you, Mr Scott, from the human inhabitants of Nerium. The ones that are currently afraid of you. The ones that believe that the best thing to do is, get rid of you." She added, almost daring him to question the need for a barrier. "I trust that because you nearly succeeded where Mr Lawson and his friends have failed three times. You will listen to Professor Flak, and Miss Ramos here. And not fly too high?" He nodded at her. "Good. Get something to eat and rest in your room Mr Scott." She looked to Tala. "Miss Ramos and your friends will catch you up with the events of the last few days."

As soon as Amelie and Ajit saw the two of them walk into the main hall, they left their place in the queue for gruel and ran towards him. Amelie hugged him tight. "Thank goodness you're ok." She said into his shoulder.

"Yeah, what happened up there?" Ajit asked.

Aaron explained everything to them like he had with the head mistress, then he told them what she had said about the school barrier.

“At least we don’t have to worry about that question, like Taylor said, we’ll learn about them soon enough.” Amelie said, unconcerned by the news of another race. “At least you’re back, they wouldn’t even let us in the classroom. We didn’t even know what was happening.”

“You should have seen Tala though.” Ajit joined in, smiling proudly at Tala. “She flat out refused to leave. Screaming and shouting at Head Mistress Taylor and Professor Iaso, until they gave in.”

Aaron thought for a moment. “I think I remember that.” He began. “I remember bits of things. One of them is you shouting, ‘I am not leaving.’” He said smiling at Tala. Then he remembered some of the other things that had not made sense to him. “What else happened while I was out?” He asked the group.

“When we got to you, you were at the bottom of a massive crater.” Ajit started, looking between the two girls.

“We thought you were dead.” Amelie took over with tears in her eyes. “There was blood all over your face, and your legs and arms were going in the wrong directions.” She wiped her eyes. “We all climbed down to get to you, but me and Ajit bounced away from your shield.”

“Then we heard Head Mistress Taylor shouting.” Tala continued. “She just appeared at the top of the crater and used magic to lift you out and through a big window into the healing classroom. We climbed out and ran with her to the classroom.” She shook her head. “When we got there, Professor Iaso was already there, she tried to stop us going in. Tried to tell us to go back to our rooms, that’s when I was shouting at her, telling her I wasn’t going anywhere.” She chuckled lightly. “Head Mistress Taylor looked a bit shocked at how angry I was with them both and she let me stay, but she told me not to get in the way of the healers.”

“But we weren’t allowed in, they told us to go back to our rooms and closed the door in our faces. We ignored them and waited in the corridor.” Ajit added.

“The healers all tried to get close to you, but they kept bouncing off your shield.” Tala carried on. “That’s when I told them that I had got to you at the bottom of the crater. They couldn’t do anything to heal you, and all I could do was clean the blood off your face and head.” She reached up and ran a hand through his hair. “They kept looking at your head and, a few hours later they noticed that you were healing yourself. But very slowly.” She looked to the other two. “Later that night I was falling asleep in the chair next to you, Professor Iaso and another Healer were in chairs nodding off as well. When we heard loud bangs in the corridor.”

“That was us getting blasted with air attacks.” Amelie explained. “We were asleep, and something woke me up, I looked down the corridor and saw that Rebecca girl coming towards us. You remember her? The second year that talks a lot, she told us how the rooms were inside the walls.” Aaron nodded. “I asked if she was ok and she just blasted us, I think I got knocked out because I don’t remember anything after that.”

“Professor Iaso told us all not to move and to be quiet.” Tala carried on. “I guess Healers don’t have much in the way of defensive magic.” She shrugged. “The door burst open, and we got hit with air magic, that girl ran to you and tried to stab you with a knife. She bounced off your shield and flew back out of the door.”

“As I was recovering from her blast that knocked Amelie out.” Ajit took over. “I saw Head Mistress Taylor come running down the stairs from her office. She asked what was going on just as the girl flew backwards out of the door. I shouted at her to get her, and she did. After the Healing professors explained what had happened, she really laid into the girl. Asked her what had got into her, she just said that she saw an opportunity and she took it. She’s in detention now.”

“Everyone else seemed actually concerned about you.” Amelie added.

Aaron shook his head in confusion. “Rebecca? She seemed ok when we spoke to her.” He said to Amelie, she nodded. “Like she’d had far too much caffeine, but she seemed ok.”

“Turns out she’s friends with some of Dylan’s friends. It sounds like he’s convincing more and more people.” She answered him sadly.

Aaron shook his head, it sounded as though the next time Dylan attacked him, there was going to be a lot more attackers to deal with.

26

That night, Aaron was laid in bed next to Tala. After four days of sitting next to his unconscious body, she had passed out as soon as her head had hit the pillow. But, after four days of being unconscious, Aaron was not tired in the slightest. He laid there trying not to think about everything that had happened while he was sleeping, he tried not to think about the fact that even unconscious, he had created a shield surrounding his body that even the professors could not get through. He tried to not think about the fact that he had healed himself without knowing, without thinking about it. He tried not to think about the fact that someone new had tried to kill him, someone he had spoken to that very day.

That last fact that he was trying not to think about, worried him. How many people had Dylan convinced? How many people would he have to face the next time he was attacked? He shook his head, he was not going to get any sleep lying there thinking about all of that.

He got up and walked into his library, the magical torches lighting themselves as he entered. He sat on his sofa in his underwear, telling himself to think about something else, anything else. As he sat there staring into space his thoughts wandered to the fall. His fall through the sky, how scared he was, how much he was panicking, how he knew he was going to die. His thoughts went backwards to when he thought he was asleep in his room, and he woke up and first realised that he was falling.

The far away screaming that he now knew was Tala, how he wondered why it was windy in his room, how he couldn't find his bedsheets, how he had woken up to see the ground and sky flashing and merging into one.

As he sat there, Aaron's brows furrowed, that wasn't how it had happened. He hadn't just woken up, he had been woken up by a voice. Someone had spoken to him. Shouted at him, inside his mind. Isabella Lockton had shouted at him and told him to wake up.

He needed to talk to the painting of her to find out how she had done that, how she had known he was in trouble and why she had saved him when she had not been overly impressed by him the last time he had spoken to her. He stood up and opened a portal to the painting room, he was about to step through when he remembered he was only wearing his underwear. He closed the portal and walked back into his bedroom to get dressed.

"Hey, what's wrong? Where are you going?" Tala's tired voice asked him as he was getting dressed.

"Sorry, I didn't mean to wake you up." He said as he walked over to kiss her. "I can't sleep, so I thought I'd go to the painting room and see if I can get any answers this time."

She looked questioningly at him. "Are you sure you're ok?"

"I'm fine, I promise." He smiled at her. "Go back to sleep, you need it."

“Ok.” She said finally. “Just don’t stay in there all night, you need sleep as well.”

“I won’t, and I’ll try not to wake you up when I get back into bed.” He kissed her again.

“I don’t mind you waking me up as long as you’re climbing into bed next to me.” She said smiling as she watched him stand up and leave the room.

“In that case, I definitely won’t be in there all night.” He winked at her and left the bedroom.

Aaron smiled as he was pulling on his robes in the library. Whenever he spoke to Tala, he was reminded how happy she made him, how he was happy that he had been brought to Nerium. Whenever Tala was involved, he didn’t even care that he was an All-Power and the world was out to get him, Tala seemed to make it all worthwhile.

He opened the portal again and stepped through. He looked around the room once he was inside, nothing had changed. He walked to his own painting, he had not paid much attention to it the last time he was in there. Suddenly curious, he looked up at his own image, staring blankly back at him. “What would you be able to tell me?” He asked the painting. As it had with Isabella Lockton and the mystery All-Power, smoke poured from the painting and rose up to form the shape of a person, this time, when it was finished Aaron was looking at the smoky form of his own body.

His smoky reflection smiled at him. “Well, isn’t this just the narcissists dream.” He laughed as he glided round the room. “Whenever you enter this room, my memories will be refreshed, I won’t be able to tell you anything about the past, about our predecessors. But I will remember everything that is inside your head. Even if you have forgotten it.”

Aaron nodded as he took that in. “In that case, why don’t you stay out here for a while, while I talk to Isabella.” His smoky form slowly nodded back at him. Aaron walked to the portrait of Isabella Lockton. “Can I ask you a question?” He asked and waited while the smoke bellowed out and into the form of Isabella Lockton.

“To summon us from our paintings, Aaron Scott. All you need to do is look at the painting, from anywhere within the room and simply say our name. You do not need to ask the painting a question before we are out here.” She said, sounding irritated as she glided around the smoky Aaron, who just stood unmoved by her presence. “What is your question?”

“How did you save my life from in here?” He asked her, getting straight to the point.

Her smoky form stopped gliding and turned to stare at him, a look of genuine confusion on her smoky face. “I have not saved your life, you must be confused.”

Aaron turned to look at his own smoky face. “Why don’t you tell her?”

Aaron listened as his smoky reflection explained everything, to Aarons relief he even included the fact that Isabella's own voice had shouted at him inside his mind to wake him up as he plummeted to the ground.

When he was finished explaining, Isabella glided to Aaron. "So, you nearly killed yourself with your own stupidity?"

Aaron stood chewing the inside of his cheek. "Looking back at it. Yes, that's exactly what happened, I was stupid, and I paid for it." He admitted, seeing no reason to hide anything from the paintings in this room.

She looked surprised and, a little impressed with his candor. "I am afraid that I cannot answer your question. I do not know, it was not me that you heard."

Aaron shook his head. "If I didn't hear your voice, then who did I hear?"

"You misunderstand me, Aaron Scott. You did hear my voice. If you had heard another's voice and simply mistook it for mine." She turned to look at the version of Aaron from the painting. "He would have said so." She turned back to Aaron. "He said that you heard my voice. I believe you did, but it was not from me."

"How can I have heard you, if it wasn't you?"

She looked around the room. “The paintings within this room, are the memories of the dead. Your own painting, as he has informed you, is refreshed whenever you enter this room. My painting, has not been refreshed for quite some time.”

Aaron was confused, he looked to his own smoky form. “Any idea what she means?”

The duplicate Aaron nodded. “Isabella Lockton did not die in the year 176. Isabella Lockton lives still. You read that in your All-Power history book.”

Aarons eyes widened. “She really shed her body? She’s really still out there?” The smoky Isabella smiled and nodded to him. “The real, living Isabella Lockton saved my life. Wow.” He ran his hands through his hair as he took this in. “Ok, that’s, insane. But, ok.” He nodded. “I have one more question for this visit.” He looked to the smoky Isabella. “If you don’t mind.” She smiled and nodded, she seemed to appreciate it when he showed her respect and honesty, so he decided to use it. “The last time I was here.” He looked toward the painting of the mystery All-Power. “I found out that there was a being that only you and our mystery friend over there have known. Could you tell me how you knew this being?”

"Ah yes. This may raise more questions for you however." She began, smiling. "When I arrived with the first humans on Nerium. Like our friend." She nodded towards the mystery All-Power. "Time was frozen, the being was there. They told me what was happening, they told me that, for a thousand years they had brought beings from another planet here and given them magical powers. And now they had decided to bring humans here, they wanted to introduce a new magical species to the planet to see what would happen. They had become bored with just the old species, when they first brought the other species here, they gave them equal magical abilities. When they brought humans to Nerium, they wanted to create a divide, just to see what would happen. They created us, the All-Powers." She looked to Aaron, a strange, vicious smile spread across her smoky face. "The being brought us to Nerium, because they were bored, they wanted multiple magical species to inhabit this world. It was the only time I ever saw them, and as far as I know. Only two of us has ever seen them."

Aaron nodded. "I will be asking about the other species that came before us, next time I come to this room." He looked between both of the smoky forms in front of him. "Thank you, both of you, for entertaining my questions."

He stood and watched as both smoky forms nodded and returned to their frames then walked to the door that was actually one of his bookshelves.

Aaron opened the door and stepped back through into his library, questions racing through his mind. He walked back into his bedroom to find Tala had woken up from the noise of the door opening into his library. She was staring at him with a cheeky smile, as he smiled back at her she flung the covers off the bed and beckoned him to her. One look at her and he pushed all of his questions to the back of his mind.

After Tala had gone back to sleep, all of the questions that Aaron had pushed to the back of his mind forced their way to the forefront again. How many species had this being brought here? Was Nerium the only planet that they brought people to? At least he finally knew how humans had first been brought to this planet, of course, he could never tell anyone, he had no proof. No one would believe him, he could not take anyone into the room to prove it and he had no way of contacting the being. Then there was the fact that Isabella Lockton had saved his life, not the painting version of her, but the real Isabella Lockton that everyone thought had died centuries ago. She had spoken in his mind, just like Tala and Amelie could.

'Isabella?'. He asked in his mind. *'Miss Lockton?'*. He waited, but there was nothing but silence in return. He shook his head, it seemed as though he had no way of contacting Isabella Lockton either.

He got up again, careful not to wake Tala, and walked back into his library. Curious to see if anything had changed, he picked up *An accurate history of The All-Power* and flicked through the pages to the beginning of his own chapter.

Aaron Scott 763 –

From the moment of Aaron Scott's arrival at Doctrina he faced the paranoia of the professors and immediately knew he was special.

Aaron Scott showed great potential upon his arrival at Doctrina surviving multiple attacks uninjured. Aaron Scott was extremely powerful, learning quickly and even teaching two dual mages things that no other dual mage had ever achieved.

The Prime Mage of the time – Prime Mage Reid ordered surveillance on Aaron Scott, the moment he learnt of the emergence of a new All-Power. The lesser Prime Mage even going as far as to visit Doctrina to threaten Aaron Scott.

After an accident Aaron Scott showed his raw power, even when he was close to death and unconscious Aaron Scott protected his body with a shield so strong that not one lesser mage could penetrate, even protecting himself against yet another attack against his life. Aaron Scott healed his own injuries rather than allow a lesser mage to treat him.

Before the end of his first year at Doctrina, Aaron Scott showed that he could become the most powerful All-Power in Neriums history.

Aaron sat staring at the page, suddenly wishing that he had not been curious. The page had changed, it was still twisting things, but that was not what was bothering him.

For months he had convinced himself that he had beaten his dreams, he had taught Amelie, Tala, Ajit, and Professor Flak how to create a sphere shield. But, on the page in front of him, it said what it had said in his second dream.

Aaron Scott was extremely powerful, learning quickly and even teaching two dual mages things that no other dual mage had ever achieved.

There it was, two dual mages, not the four dual mages that he had taught how to create the sphere shield. Aaron sat there confused, why did everything give him more questions?

"What are you doing out here?" Tala asked, waking Aaron. He was sat on the sofa, he still had *An accurate history of The All-Power* open in his lap.

"I still couldn't sleep, so I came out here to see what this book said about me now." He told her what his new page said and then looked up to see her smirking at him.

"I'm sorry, I can't take you seriously like that." She said with a cheeky smile.

Aaron looked down and realised that he was sat there in his underwear, his underwear that the book was covering. "One track mind." He laughed as he closed the book and stood up and walked back into his bedroom to get dressed.

"Are you complaining?" He heard her ask.

"Not even a little bit." He laughed as she followed him back into the bedroom.

"That is strange." Amelie said after Aaron explained what his new page said over breakfast.

Aaron turned to Tala. "That's the right response."

She rolled her eyes at him. "She wouldn't have responded like that if you were nearly naked."

"I think I might have had a few questions if that was happening." Ajit laughed. "Maybe you could ask the paintings about the book when you go back."

"I could, but it will have to wait until the Autumn Celebration break, I've already been for this break." He told them all that he had learnt in the room.

"You never mentioned that you heard Lockton's voice." Amelie said once he had finished.

"I'd forgotten about it, until I tried to go to sleep." He told her honestly.

"But it wasn't the painting?" Tala asked, Aaron shook his head. "So, is she just energy floating around? Or is she a ghost?"

"Maybe she was telling the truth and she is actually a god." Ajit added.

Aaron shook his head. "She isn't a god. I think Tala's right. I think that she shed her body and now she's energy."

Amelie shook her head. "Whatever she is. Energy, ghost, God. It doesn't matter, she saved your life." She looked at Aaron smiling, her eyes brimming with fresh tears. Aaron smiled back at her, hiding his surprise, it was the first time she had not called Isabella Lockton a maniac or a lunatic or something worse. "At least you got an answer to why we were first brought here. Not that you can do anything with that information though." She said as she looked away.

As Tala and Ajit continued to debate whether Isabella Lockton was a ghost or a god, Aaron spoke to Amelie within his mind. *'Are you OK?'* He asked her.

She was quiet for so long that Aaron was beginning to wonder if she had heard him. *'Yeah.'* Her voice finally rang in his head. *'It's just, it's been a really long time since I had friends like the three of you.'* She looked at him and quickly looked away. Aaron saw that she had tears running down her face. *'I really care about you all. I don't want to lose you three.'*

He smiled at her. *'None of us are going anywhere.'* He said as he bumped his shoulder into hers. *'And I promise not to be an idiot and fly into barriers again.'*

Later that morning, the four of them were back at the tree. Aaron stood looking out to the rolling hills surrounding the school. “Head Mistress Taylor said that the school grounds go on for ten miles in every direction, didn’t she?” He said looking at Tala, she nodded. He looked back out at the hills. “We’ve been here nearly seven months, that’s almost a whole year here.” He turned back to his friends. “And we have only seen the classrooms, the common room, and this tree. Anyone want to go exploring the grounds?”

Ajit looked over the hills. “Why, there’s nothing there.” He said pointing out at them.

“That’s just one direction.” Aaron laughed. “Choose whichever direction you want.”

Tala smiled. “I’m in.” She hopped over to stand next to Ajit and linked her arm in his. “Come on. Choose a direction.”

He looked to Amelie, with a hopeful look on his face. “Sorry, I think we should go as well.” She said shaking her head. “A change of scenery would be nice.”

Ajit shook his head. “Fine.” He said, giving in, he turned on the spot and pointed back towards the school. “That way.”

“Back to school?” Tala asked.

Ajit rolled his eyes at her. “No. Behind the school, that way is just hills.” He pointed away from the school. “I don’t think I’ve ever even seen behind the school.”

“There are some woods in that direction.” Aaron said as they set off walking round the school. “I noticed them before I hit the barrier.”

They walked for nearly two hours before they reached the woods that Aaron had seen from the air. Amelie and Tala walking and laughing together.

Aaron had listened to Ajit complain the whole way. “Why can’t you open one of those green doors of yours?” He had asked Aaron.

“Because I’ve never been there.” Aaron answered shrugging his shoulders at him. “I don’t know if the doorways will work if I haven’t been there before. Why don’t you fly?”

“I can’t fly that well yet.” He said sadly. “But you went to the secret All-Power painting room through a doorway, and you’d never been there.”

Aaron looked at him. “But I had been there.” He said plainly. “I’d been there in my dream remember. If you can’t fly that well you could practice or, why not use your sphere shield?”

Ajit shrugged. “Nah, I’ll just walk.” The two of them caught up with Tala and Amelie, he looked around as they reached the tree line. “What are we looking for anyway?”

Aaron smiled at him as he put his arm around Tala. “We aren’t looking for anything.”

Amelie put her arms around Ajit’s waist. “Yeah, can’t we just enjoy a few days without learning, worrying about attacks or someone having a deadly accident?”

28

The four of them enjoyed the remainder of the Summer Celebration break incident free. Each morning, one of them picked a direction at random and set off walking. They would walk until the sun was at its highest and it was time for lunch, then they would use one of Aarons green portals to go back into his room and walk to the main hall.

“That is cool.” Tala exclaimed the first time they reappeared in Aarons room.

Amelie’s eyes lit up. “We could go anywhere.” She had said smiling.

“Why don’t you just open a portal straight into the main hall?” Ajit had asked.

Aaron thought about it for a moment. “Because, people are already scared of me. And I don’t just mean people outside of the school. The people here, that have seen me every day, they still stare at me every day. Think about it, they’re so scared of me that more and more of them are joining Dylan every time he attacks, and taking chances whenever they can. Like Rebecca did.” He shook his head. “What do you think would happen if they suddenly found out that I could open portals, and be anywhere with one step?”

After lunch every day they would go back to Aarons room, open a portal and step through to where they had walked to that morning. They would spend the afternoon out in the school grounds, practicing their defensive magics. Despite what the head mistress had said, Aaron was still expecting another attack when the third and fourth year students returned to Doctrina after their second tour of Nerium. Amelie, Tala and even Ajit agreed with him.

By the time the last day of the Summer Celebration break came around, Aaron was confident that each of his friends could defend themselves well enough that he was not as concerned with keeping them safe. He still worried about them, and was convinced that, if and when another attack came around, he would have to fight the urge to safely hide them away somewhere.

The four of them were once again sat by the tree, its leaves that just days before had been a vibrant green, already beginning to turn brown. Signalling the beginning of the end of the year. They normally sat with their backs to the school looking out at the hills that surrounded them, but not this time.

All four of them sat facing the school, watching as the older students returned. They saw Dylan and his friends being escorted passed the accommodation wing and toward the school by a group of professors, back into their detention rooms. The four of them stayed sitting under the tree, waiting for an attack until the sun was below the horizon.

“It’s getting a little chilly.” Tala said as the daylight slowly faded away.

Aaron did not reply, he just closed his eyes and searched within himself, looking for the source of his fire magic. Once he found it, he expanded it to fill him and pushed it outwards, so that heat was radiating from him, creating a bubble of warm air around his group. He opened his eyes and smiled, impressed with himself.

“That is incredible.” Tala said as she cuddled into him. On his other side Amelie moved closer and snuggled into his other arm. “It really is.” She said smiling as she felt his warmth.

“It’s not fair, is what it actually is.” Ajit said glumly.

“Why?” Amelie asked him.

“I can’t exactly cuddle into Aaron to get warm.”

“Why not?” Aaron laughed.

“We’re both boys.”

Aaron laughed at him again. “Don’t be such a prude, get in here.” The four of them sat cuddled up together for another hour. “I don’t think anyone is going to try anything tonight.” He finally admitted, relieved. They stood and started to walk back to the common room, Amelie, Ajit, and Tala all walking close to Aaron so that they could keep benefiting from the heat he was radiating.

Aaron stopped heating the air around him as the four of them entered the common room, he looked around to see the room was full. The first year and the second year students speaking with the newly returned third and fourth years, finding out whatever they could about the outside world. They saw Heidi sitting with some other Water mages and as his group of friends walked toward her through the crowded room, Aaron couldn't help but wonder, how many of them had Dylan convinced? How many of them had he managed to turn against him? How many people in that very room were just waiting for an opportunity to attack him? Like Rebecca had done.

"Relax, no one is going to attack in here." Tala said, sensing his apprehension. "There's too many people."

"Hi." Heidi said, beaming as she saw Aaron getting closer. Tala held his hand tighter, then sat on his lap once he took a seat near Heidi. "How are you? How was your break? I heard about your accident, are you OK?" She asked, paying no attention to Tala.

Aaron smiled and put his arms around Tala's waist. "I'm good. The break was nice and quiet. And I'm fine after my accident. It was my own stupid fault." He reeled off answers to her questions. "You seem happier with this tour, was it less disappointing than the last one?"

"So much happier." She answered, her eyes wide. "I told Professor Brook how disappointed I was last time, he's the third year Water mage professor." She added when she noticed Aarons confused look. "So, this time, he took us to villages where single and dual branch mages live together. There aren't many villages like that but, it's a start."

"It does sound a little better." Amelie said, joining the conversation. "It's still weird that most places refuse to live together. What are people like about Aaron now? Are they still the same?"

Heidi nodded, looking between her and Aaron, still ignoring Tala. "They heard about the last time Dylan attacked you, when you saved us all." She smiled at Aaron. "Thank you for that by the way, I never thanked you. I would not want to have been out in the open while all those attack spells were flying around." She said, still smiling at him. Aaron felt Tala shift on his lap. "Some people have heard that part and have started to change their minds. Because you protected us. Some heard that you made a giant dragon, and they are even more afraid of you." She shrugged.

As the evening dragged on the four of them sat there while Heidi and the other third years told them more stories from outside the school grounds, until people slowly started disappearing to go to bed.

"I never liked her." Tala said as Heidi walked away. "She's always been too smiley and too nice around you." She said to Aaron. "And now, we find out that she's a coward. I'm still a little mad that you hid us underground. But she's happy you did it!" She shook her head, following Heidi with her eyes. "Coward."

"Come on, she's not that bad." Aaron laughed as they all stood to go back to their rooms.

"I agree with Tala, I've never seen her talk to anyone else the way she talks to you." Amelie added. "I think she wants to stay on your good side just in case you go bad."

"Maybe she's just a nice person." Ajit added.

"Thank you." Aaron said bumping into him. "I don't want to think like that." He said to Tala and Amelie. "I'm already wondering who is going to try and attack me next. I don't want to have to wonder if someone is being nice to me, just so I don't kill them just in case I go bad."

"I still don't like her." Tala said shaking her head. "I'm going to sleep in my room tonight." She said as she reached up and wrapped her arms around his neck. "Get a full nights sleep for a change."

Aaron raised his eyebrows at her. "Are you saying I keep you awake?"

"No. I'm saying that I can't lay next to you and just go to sleep." She answered with a cheeky smile on her face.

He kissed her goodnight and walked into the All-Power corridor feeling happy. Happy that he had Tala, happy that the end of the Summer Celebration break had come and gone, with no new attacks, and happy that at least some people outside the school grounds were beginning to change their minds about him.

*

Aaron was stood in silence in his library, a silence so loud it was deafening, a silence so thick he felt as though it was smothering him. His feet moved to carry him into his corridor and out to the common room, he felt as though he was moving in slow motion. As though the silence that was smothering him was slowing his movements. He heard nothing, not his footsteps, not the swish of his robes, not his breathing. He heard nothing.

His feet carried him through his door and into the common room, he looked out into the room. It was crowded as it had been when everyone had returned from the tour of Nerium, except not one person was moving, or speaking. It was as if every single person in the common room was a statue. Aaron's feet carried him forward. He reached the frozen Amelie first, she was frozen with her finger outstretched as though she was pointing, as he got to her, she came to life.

She looked at him with an expression Aaron had never seen on her face. An expression that was undeniably lust. She slowly moved toward him, her finger still outstretched, gently placing her fingertip on his chest as she got to him, she slowly moved around him, running her finger along his body as she went.

"We are the same you and I." She said as she walked around his back and back into his field of view, her voice breaking the silence, but even her voice was in slow motion. She pressed her body against his and wrapped her arms around his neck, running her hands through his hair. She raised her lips and whispered as she nibbled his ear. "We are both killers." She moved away from him and returned to her statuesque position, with her finger outstretched.

Aaron's gaze followed her finger to see Dylan frozen in place, stood with his hands behind his back and a small smile on his face. Aaron's feet did not carry him toward him, instead Aaron watched his own hand raise and watched as he created a solid spike out of the air.
He watched as he slowly sent the spike toward Dylan, he watched as the spike gently pressed against and pierced the skin of his neck. Aaron watched as his spike slowly went into Dylan's neck and slowly pierced its way out the other side. Dylan's expression did not change as blood poured from holes in his neck. Aaron watched emotionlessly as Dylan slowly went pail as he bled to death, finally unfreezing, and collapsing to the ground. Dead.

Aaron's feet moved again and carried him towards a seated Tala, she was sat frozen with her head in her hands. As he reached her, she came to life and slowly looked up at him, tears slowly trickling down her cheeks. "How did this happen? I don't understand." She lowered her head back into her hands and froze again.

Aaron followed his feet once more, towards Ajit this time. He unfroze as Aaron got close to him, he looked to Aaron, he was as upset as Tala had been, but he didn't speak. Instead, in slow motion, the left side of his head exploded. Blood and brain slowly flying through the air. Ajit collapsed to the ground, his lifeless right eye staring up at Aaron.

Aaron looked around the room as the silence was broken once more by a loud cracking and crumbling noise, he slowly turned to stare out into the room, trying to place the noise. His eyes turned upward and he saw the entire roof of the common room falling in slow motion about to crush him and every frozen statuesque person in the room.

*

Aaron woke with a start, he quickly stood up just to check that he wasn't moving in slow motion. He let out a breath and sat back down on his bed. "What the hell was that?" He asked the empty room.

Aaron was waiting in the common room when Tala, Amelie and Ajit walked out of the dual mage corridor the next morning. He tried to look as normal as he could but failed dismally, the three of them took one look at him and stopped in their tracks.

"What's wrong with you? You look like you've seen a ghost." Ajit said as the four of them started walking to the main hall.

"You had a new dream, didn't you?" Tala said, he nodded.

“Terrifying or informative?” Amelie asked.

“Disturbing.” Aaron answered quietly. “So disturbing, I’m not even sure I want to tell you about it.”

“Don’t be weird, if you’re going through it. We’re going through it too. Right?” He added to the two girls. They both agreed. “Tell us, and leave nothing out.”

“OK, you could have left some things out.” Ajit said after Aaron had finished telling them all about his new dream, every detail of it. “Why the hell did my head explode?”

“I don’t know.”

“What was I crying about?” Tala joined in.

“I don’t know.”

“Why was I all over you?” Amelie asked quietly after a moment of silence, she had gone very pale.

“I don’t know.” Aaron looked at her, confused as to why she chose that part of her actions in the dream and not what she had said to him.

They reached the main hall and were surrounded by too many people to carry on talking about it. Aaron was thankful for this, as he wanted nothing more than to forget the whole thing.

At least the first dreams made sense, they were complete scenes. He hadn't exactly enjoyed the sensation of killing Ajit in the first dream, but it had been him doing it, he had felt rage when he had looked at Ajit and even a sense of achievement once Ajit was lying dead on the floor.

It had been strange to suddenly be thirty years older and a professor, but he felt pride in his student Caitlin, and he felt disappointment when he read his page in *An accurate history of The All-Power.*

Even in the dream in the secret room where he had spoken with Aban Fasil, he had felt irritation, he had even learnt something. In all three of the first dreams, it had been Aaron doing these things, he had felt emotions.

But, not in this new dream, he had watched from inside his body, as his body did things. Like a passenger. He had felt no emotion at all, he had felt nothing while Amelie was all over him, he had felt nothing while he slowly and gruesomely murdered Dylan, he had felt nothing while Tala was crying in front of him, and he had felt nothing while Ajit's head exploded. This new dream was, like he had told Tala, Ajit, and Amelie, disturbing.

He could not focus on History of Nerium, but that was not anything new, and not completely because of the dream. Professor Horton had been droning on about the founding of settlements for months, Aaron had stopped listening in his class months ago. When he got to Air Fire Classroom one after Professor Horton had finally finished, he was eager to move on to learning something new.

"Good morning everyone, I trust you enjoyed the Summer Celebration break." She looked at Aaron. "After your recovery of course." Aaron attempted to smile, and she continued. "Miss Durand, Miss Ramos, Mr Shah please continue practicing for a moment." They nodded and spread out across the classroom, each beginning to hover, with varying degrees of success. Aaron noticed that, for the first time, Ajit was doing better than the two girls. "Now, Mr Scott. Why don't you show me how you are getting on with voice projection?" She said as she lifted off the ground and flew to the other side of the room. "Go ahead." She said quietly once she had landed, but Aaron heard her as though she was standing next to him.

"I think I'm doing OK." He said quietly, using the air to carry the vibrations of his voice across the room and to the ears of Professor Flak. "Am I ready to move onto something new?" He asked quietly.

"I would say so." He heard her voice as though she was stood next to him, he thought he could detect the tiniest hint of a smile on her voice. She flew back across the room to join him. "And I have been giving that some thought. Have you noticed that every time you have been attacked, Head Mistress Taylor has arrived extremely quickly?"

Aaron thought for a moment, he had not noticed that, but now that he was thinking about it. It was a little strange, how had he not noticed before. “No, I hadn’t noticed. How does she always know?” He had a sudden sinking feeling, questioning the head mistress. Was she behind all the attacks? How else could she know about them so quickly? If the head mistress was orchestrating the attacks, then why had she appeared to stop them all? Why had she not just let them kill him?

“Since your arrival here, Head Mistress Taylor has taken to monitoring the vibrations in the air. Constantly searching for signs of attack.”

Aaron let out a breath he hadn’t noticed that he had been holding. Head Mistress Taylor had not been behind the attacks on his life.

“The Head Mistress has informed me that you are able to sense anger from your attackers.” Professor Flak continued. “That is an extremely useful ability to have, when your attackers are attacking you.” She glanced towards his friends. “But what if they are attacking someone else. To get to you.”

She went on to explain how to use the very same vibrations he had learnt to use to carry his voice, to sense malicious magics.

This made Aaron happy, he had something he could focus on. He could focus on learning this new ability, he could use learning how to sense attacks on the air as a distraction to keep his mind from the new dream.

A distraction. That was exactly what he needed, he needed to keep himself so busy that he did not even have time to think about this new and disturbing dream.

For the next few weeks that is what Aaron did, he threw himself into studying and into practicing. Professor Flak had begun with teaching him how to identify different people and their unique vibrations on the air.

"Once I am able to identify different people." Aaron had said after the professor had begun teaching him that. "Would I be able to use what we have just learnt to project my voice to them? If I needed to."

"You could indeed." She had answered with a wide smile. "In fact, that is how many Air mages communicate over distance. Of course, it is only a useful form of communication between two, or more, Air mages. You could pass a message onto a mage from a different branch, of course, but they would not be able to answer."

Thanks to throwing himself into his studies, he had finally started making progress in his Earth Air class, the pillars he had been attempting to grow out of the ground for the last few months were finally beginning to stabilise and not crumbling into dust the moment he stopped concentrating on them.

Professor Stein had moved him on to creating rain and sunshine. "Obviously we cannot control the weather." He had said to Aaron, after he had assessed his ability to heat the air and evaporate raindrops. "But we can reproduce certain aspects within a small area. As it only rains in the season of autumn and can get extremely sunny during the summer months. These two separate yet similar abilities are very useful, especially when it comes to growing crops. These abilities are usually used together with an Earth mage. The Earth mage helps the crops to grow from within the ground while we assist with the nutrients needed from the sun and the rain." He smiled at Aaron. "You probably won't need another mage to assist you. But the rest of us do."

Even with throwing himself into his studies, Aaron still struggled with underwater breathing. He had managed to pull air from the water, but only for around five minutes. He still could not perform this ability well enough to move on to something new. Aaron found this extremely annoying, why could he not manage to perfect this ability when so many others were coming to him so much easier.

"Here we are Mr Scott, your very last weekly interview as a first year student." Head Mistress Taylor said as he sat down in one of the armchairs in her office. "How are you finding your studies?"

Aaron nodded, considering his progress throughout the year. “I’m enjoying most of my lessons.” He began. “I feel like Air and Fire magics are easier. I’m making progress with Professor Flak and Professor Stein.” The head mistress nodded. “I’m making a little progress with Earth magic, my pillars are slowly getting stronger. But I don’t feel like I’m doing well with Water magic, I’ve been stuck on the same thing for the last two terms.” He finished, shaking his head, annoyed with himself.

“Underwater breathing takes every water and dual mage quite a while to perfect. As I have mentioned before, the fact that you are struggling with certain magics is easing some fears in people outside these grounds.” Head Mistress Taylor smiled kindly. “But don’t forget how quickly you mastered control of water and ice. Try not to see one setback as a failure.” She smiled at Aaron again. “As this is the end of your first year, it also means that the third years will be leaving. This, of course, includes Mr Lawson and the majority of his friends that have been living in the detention halls for most of this year.” She looked concerned. “This means that they will be attending the end of year feast in the common room. There will be professors posted outside just in case. We cannot enter, the door is magically sealed to all but students.” She took a long breath as she considered Aaron. “I do not believe that they will attempt to harm you with so many other young mages, and their own friends, within the common room. But I would like you to be vigilant, in case I am wrong.”

Aaron walked through the school corridors after the interview and before the rest of the students finished their lessons. As he walked, he considered what the head mistress had said, he agreed with her.

Dylan wanted to stop him, Aaron. He had tried to get Tala, Amelie, and Ajit the second time he had attacked, but only to stop Aaron. He wouldn't risk hurting all the other students, would he?

As he turned left out of the courtyard, he saw the second year Air mages going in and out of the common room, each floating a tray or two of food that the professors had collected for the Autumn Celebration feast. As he reached the door into the common room, he saw the table set in the centre of the room and the masses of food left to be transported inside.

"Can I help?" He asked Professor Squall, the second year Air Professor.

The professor smiled at him. "Of course, Mr Scott. Many hands make light work and all that."

Aaron looked between the trays left to be carried into the common room and the table waiting for them. "Everyone, stand out of the way." He shouted to the second year Air mage students. He looked back to the food waiting to be moved and focussed on the air underneath the trays, at once, all the trays lifted into the air and carried themselves into the common room and laid neatly on the table. Once he had finished, he smiled at himself, proud of how well he could control the air.

“Incredibly impressive Mr Scott.” Professor Squall said, breaking into Aaron’s self-congratulatory thoughts. Aaron looked around to see all the second year mages looking shocked at how easily he had unloaded the professor’s cart. “I wonder who will be unloading every feast next year.” He added with a smile as he wheeled the cart away.

Aaron walked into the common room, all the second years were still staring at him. “Sorry.” He said, unsure why he was apologising.

One of them laughed, breaking the others out of their shock. “What for? You just saved us half an hour of walking back and forth. How did you do that?”

Aaron shrugged. “The same way you do it I suppose, Air magic just comes really easy to me.” He said, warily looking through the second years.

“Cool, I’m Ben. I’m going to be one of the prefects next year.” He said kindly as he held out a hand to Aaron.

Aaron shook his hand. “Guessing I don’t have to introduce myself.”

Ben laughed again. “No, definitely not.” He looked around his classmates. “None of us are Dylan’s friends by the way.” He added smiling at Aaron.

“Am I that obvious?” Aaron asked with a little chuckle.

Ben tilted his head to one side. “You’re looking around at us all, like you’re trying to work out who’s going to attack you.” Aaron nodded. “Trust me, we are far more impressed by you than scared of you.” The others in the room nodded and muttered their agreement as they moved to arrange the trays of food that Aaron had just brought in. “Are you that good with all magic?”

Aaron shook his head. “No, I’m not great with Earth magic and I’m really bad at Water magic.”

“I bet you’re better at them than I am.” Ben laughed again. “Normally there are dual mages to help with this bit.” He said as he looked around the common room. “But all the dual mages in our year are Earth Water mages.” He looked back to Aaron. “And hey, we only have one more to set up and then it’s your turn for a year.” He smiled again.

Aaron was not sure why, but he liked this Ben. He seemed genuinely happy and friendly. He spent the next hour helping the second years arrange the feast and rearrange the common room ready for when everyone else finished their lessons.

When lessons finished, the first to walk into the common room were Tala, Amelie, and Ajit. Their classroom was the furthest away, but the three of them had become so skilled at flying that they had taken to flying out from the open air classroom and down to the common room.

Tala came skipping over to Aaron as soon as she saw him. “We’re not first years anymore.” She said happily.

“Technically we are, until the new first years get here.” Amelie said as she reached Aaron.

“Yeah but, no more learning as first years.” Ajit added happily.

The rest of the first and second year students slowly filled the common room over the next hour. They all sat eating and laughing, enjoying the start of the Autumn Celebration break that marked the end of the year.

Aaron had positioned himself so he had a clear view of the entrance door. An hour after the last second year, the first of the third years arrived. It was Heidi, she led the third years into the common room, smiling as she came. Aaron saw Dylan and his friends enter, but he felt no anger coming from him, Aaron relaxed slightly. After another hour with everyone chatting and laughing, the noise of conversation in the room had risen to a loud roar, it reminded Aaron of the bar he had been in on his last night on Earth, he smiled at the memory as he stood and walked away from his group of friends and to the table at the centre of the room to get some more food.

As he turned to leave the table. He saw Dylan stood ten feet away from him, he was stood still, with a small smile on his face, with his hands behind his back, staring at Aaron. Exactly as he had been in Aaron’s dream. Aaron stared back at him for a moment, waiting for him to say something but he didn’t, he just stood there, smiling.

Then Aaron heard something over the roar of conversation, something else from his dream, he heard cracking and crumbling. With sudden realisation he looked up, he dropped the food he had collected as he saw the entire roof of the common room come free and start falling. Falling to crush every person enjoying the feast.

Aaron raised his hands as others noticed the roof falling in on them. He pushed the air above him with all his might, he dropped to one knee as he caught and stopped the roof from falling and managed to put his shield up just as he heard Dylan shout into the room.

“Now!”

Aaron felt attack spells bounce from his shield, but he did not dare look down, he was still concentrating on not dropping the roof and crushing every student in the school. He felt someone run to stand next to him, then he felt the effort of holding the roof diminish, he risked a glance next to him. Ben, the second year Air mage had jumped to help him. He felt the weight of the roof lessen more, he looked to his other side and saw Tala next to him, straining with the effort it was taking for her to hold the roof. All the while, attack spells were bouncing off their three shields. With the three of them holding the roof, Aaron risked a look around. Amelie was close by, on her knees helping someone that had been hurt. There were fires catching all around the common room and a lot of people were screaming.

"Fire mages." Aaron shouted, using the air to make his voice louder. The screaming quietened as his voice filled the room. "Put the fires out. Earth mages, build pillars to hold the roof." He looked directly at Dylan. "Dylan stop this, tell your friends to stop. You are going to kill everyone."

"I told you when you got here. I am going to stop you."

Aaron swore loudly, the air amplifying his voice. "I haven't done anything you idiot. You are the one that is about to kill three hundred people. Including yourself, you absolute moron." He shook his head and felt the vibrations in the air, searching for Head Mistress Taylor.

He found her, she was just outside the common room. He used the air to carry his voice to her ears. "Head Mistress, Dylan has attacked. I can't hold this much longer." He looked around again to see pillars slowly growing around the room and Fire mages trying to put fires out, but they were also trying to dodge the attacks that were still bouncing off his shield. Amelie was still helping the injured person and he could hear a lot of people screaming behind him.

"I know, Mr Scott, we are outside, but we cannot enter. The door is sealed to us." Head Mistress Taylors panicked voice reached his ears.

"Lift it." Ben said next to Aaron, he had heard the head mistress's voice as well. Aaron looked to Tala, she was sweating from the effort of just holding the roof. She looked back at him and nodded.

"Head Mistress, look up." Aaron said as he, Tala and Ben all screamed as they used every bit of energy they could without shutting their shields off. Frustratingly slowly the roof lifted higher than the walls and slowly lifted high enough for someone to fit through. Head Mistress Taylor came into view with other flyers, each of them carrying other non-flying mages. The Earth mage professors assisting with building and strengthening the pillars before they reached the ground, the other professors working to restrain Dylan and his friends. Aaron, Tala, and Ben lowered the roof as soon as the pillars were high enough. The three of them dropped to their knees when the roof was supported.

Aaron was staring at the ground. "Thank you." He said to the two of them, he looked up just in time to see Tala launch herself toward Dylan. Dylan had already been restrained as had all the other attackers, but Tala did not seem to care. She ran straight to him and punched him to the ground, she climbed on top of him and continued punching every part of him that she could get to until Aaron reached her and pulled her away from him.

"Get these idiots out of here." Head Mistress Taylor shouted to the other professors that had the attackers restrained. Sounding much angrier than Aaron had ever heard her. "Earth professors, get your students and rebuild the roof. Healers, see to any wounded." She left the common room, dragging Dylan away.

Tala was still struggling in Aarons arms trying to get to Dylan. "He should die. I'm going to kill him." She was screaming.

“Tala!” Aaron said. “Calm down, it’s over.”

She went limp in his arms, she looked up to him and he saw her face was wet with tears. “Ajit.”

“What about him?” He asked, looking around. “Where is he?”

She didn’t answer, instead she broke from his arms and ran to help Amelie with the injured person. Aaron followed to see what he could do to help. He stopped when he got close enough to see the injured person.

Amelie was sat cradling Ajit. The left side of his head was missing. His lifeless right eye was staring up at Aaron.

Ajit was laying in Amelie’s arms dead, there was no way to heal him from an injury like that.

Tala was sat with her head in her hands, she looked up at Aaron, tears streaming down her face. “I don’t understand, how did this happen.”

Aaron looked back to Ajit’s body. Then to Amelie cradling him. Then he heard her voice in his head.

‘They did this Aaron.’ She looked up at him. *‘They killed him.’*

He nodded at her, felt for the vibrations of Head Mistress Taylor, and stepped backwards into a green portal.

He stepped out in front of the school doors just before the professors and his attackers, Ajit's killers, walked into the courtyard. They stopped as they saw him stood in front of them.

"Mr Scott." Head Mistress Taylor said surprised. "How did you get here so fast?"

Aaron stared at Dylan as she held him. "They killed Ajit head mistress." He watched Dylan as he said that, he showed no emotion.

"Mr Scott." The head mistress said, sounding nervous.

"You were willing to kill everyone in that room." Aaron said with forced composure to Dylan.

"Mr Scott, I think you need to calm down." The head mistress continued.

"I am calm, head mistress."

"I didn't want to kill anyone other than you. You need to be stopped."

"You really are bloody stupid, aren't you." Aaron replied, without moving he hardened the air in front of him to form a spike. "You had your friends bring the roof down to distract me." He slowly sent the spike towards Dylan. "What do you think would have happened if you had managed to kill me?"

“You would have died, and I would have stopped the All-Power menace.”

“I would have dropped the roof you idiot.” The spike reached Dylan and gently pressed its tip into his neck. “I would have dropped the roof and every single person in there would be dead right now.” Dylan had realised that Aaron had an invisible weapon pressing into his neck. “Including you.”

“Aaron!” Head Mistress Taylor shouted, as a small droplet of blood trickled down Dylan’s neck.

Aarons eyes flicked to her, it was the first time she had not called him Mr Scott, he looked back to Dylan. “I could have killed you at any point this year, Dylan. But I am not like you. I could kill you and all of your friends right now. But I am not like you.” He dropped his control of the spike and it returned to nothing but air. “I am not a murderer.” He took a step towards Dylan. “You are.” He spat at him. “I don’t know what the justice system is like on this planet, but I hope they have the death sentence.” He said, his anger finally making it to his voice. “You just murdered my best friend, you deserve it.”

30

There had been other injuries, cuts and bruises, a few broken bones and quite a few burns. But Ajit was the only one that had died. The Healer professors and their students had seen to the injuries.

The Earth professors had repaired the roof, and their students had cleared all the rubble out of the common room.

Thanks to the confusion in the room, no one had noticed Aaron stepping into his green portal. Tala had needed healing as she had burst her eardrum from the effort of protecting everyone else. Amelie had not said a word.

She had not said a word as Ajit was buried in the grounds, close to the tree that the four of them had spent so much time under. She had not said a word as Professor Hawthorn had grown a rose bush that would never whither from Ajit's new grave. She had not said a word when Head Mistress Taylor had told the three of them what was going to happen.

"Mr Lawson and his accomplices have been taken to jail. They will be charged with endangering life and the Murder of Mr Shah. Of Ajit." The head mistress had said sadly. "They will be in jail for a long time. I assure you all, they will see justice."

“I wish she’d talk to us.” Tala said a few days after the attack. “Do you think she’s going to be OK?”

Aaron nodded. “She’ll talk when she’s ready, we just have to be there for her when she is.”

The other students in the common room had all become a lot friendlier to Aaron, every one of them was grateful that he had saved their lives. He had told every one of them that he had not done it alone, that it was only thanks to Tala and Bens help that he had managed to hold the roof long enough for pillars to be built to support it.

It had been eight days since the attack. Since Ajit’s death. Aaron and Tala watched as Amelie walked away from them.

‘I need to talk to you.’ Amelie’s voice rang in Aaron’s head. *‘I’m at his grave.’*

“She wants to talk to me.” He told Tala, tapping the side of his head.

“Go.” She nodded. “Call me when I can come too.” She said tapping the side of her own head.

Amelie was sat by the tree, close to Ajit’s grave, staring out to the hills when Aaron got there. He sat down next to her and waited until she was ready. The two of them sat together in silence for a long time.

“We were.” She began, her voice cracking from underuse. She cleared her throat. “We were laughing and then a piece of the roof fell on him. All of a sudden, he was stood in front of me, with half of his head gone.” She wiped her eyes, Aaron sat next to her, tears running down his own face. “He was still smiling, then his smile went away. And the light in his eyes was gone.”

Aaron put his arm around her, and she leaned into him as she cried.

“I fell to the ground with him. He was in my arms before he hit the ground.” Amelie cleared her throat again and wiped her eyes. “Before we came here.” She sat up straight and looked back out to the hills. “Before we came here, I was in jail.” She stopped as if she was waiting for Aaron to say something, he did not. He just waited for her to continue. “I got married when I was twenty three. I was too young. He was an arsehole. He didn’t even let me go to my parents’ funerals, he stopped me having any friends. He used to beat me. For fifteen years I made excuses for it, thought I loved him, thought he loved me. Then one day I’d had enough. I thought I’d planned it perfectly. When the police came, I was holding his body pretending to be heartbroken. But they figured me out. I went to jail for murdering my husband, it didn’t matter that he had tortured me for fifteen years. I went to jail.” She turned to look at Aaron. “That’s why I made Ajit and Tala come out with me to meet you. Everyone we spoke to kept saying that All-Powers were the strongest mages. I wanted to be friends with the strongest person I could find.” She said with fresh tears filling her eyes.

"That's changed now, I'm friends with you because you are a good person." She shook her head. "No. I'm not friends with you, I love you. Not like I loved Ajit, but I love you and I love Tala. You three are the best friends I've ever had." She looked towards Ajit's rose bush. "You two, now. I'm sorry."

Aaron shook his head. "Don't be. It doesn't matter why you came out to meet me, I'm glad you did. I feel the same way. I love all three of you." He looked to Ajit's rose bush as well. "He was an idiot, but he was our idiot. And I loved him too."

She smiled and leaned back into him. "I'm going to tell Tala all of that too. But I won't tell her the next part." She rested her head on his shoulder. "I don't want justice. I want them to die. I want revenge. I want you to help me kill them. I want you to learn everything you possibly can from the paintings in that room. And I want them dead."

Aaron held her tightly. "I've already started thinking about it." He admitted. "They will die, every one of them. But we have to be patient, we have to play the game of school. When we finish here. You and I will make sure they pay."

She nodded as she leaned into him. "I'm sick of being the one that gets abused. I'm sick of being the one that gets hurt. Whatever happens. Whether we do it quietly or you end up like every other All-Power. I will be right there next to you, Aaron."

"I will go to the room for every single self-study session I have." He said as he stroked her hair. "But, for now. We play the game. We will be perfect students, even if people attack us again next year. Are we clear?"

"Crystal." She nodded.

He nodded too. "Let me know when you're ready for Tala to come out here, she's desperate to talk to you."

Tala had listened as Amelie told her about her life before Nerium and then launched herself into Amelie's arms. "I'd have helped you plan it, so you didn't go to jail." She had said to her. Amelie and Aaron did not tell her about the rest of their conversation.

Aaron woke up on the last Friday of the Autumn Celebration break, the day the new first years would arrive. He got dressed and left his room, as soon as he left his corridor into the common room, he stopped. Confused.

The day before, his room, along with the rooms of everyone else in his year were on the wall to the left of the entrance, all of their rooms were now on the wall opposite the entrance. The wall to the left was now blank, and door free.

“Oh, good. You’re awake.” Ben’s voice came from the entrance. Aaron looked towards him. “Oh, yeah. You’re a second year now.” He chuckled as he noticed Aaron’s confusion. “That’s where the second year rooms are. The first year doors will open up here when each branch is filled.” He said laughing and pointing to where Aaron’s door had been the day before. “Until then, would you mind helping us with the food again?”

Aaron nodded and helped, meaning he brought all of the food in. As the new third years set about arranging it all he turned to Ben. “Isn’t it a little early for a feast?”

Ben smiled. “This is food for the whole day. Remember when you woke up in the hall when you got here? Well, we can’t really go to the hall for meals. So we just sit here, watching that wall as the new people discover what branches they are and we celebrate when they all get in here.” He looked to Aaron. “Normally it’s a loud happy celebration. Not like it was when you got here.”

“Ajit’s room is gone.” Tala told Aaron once her and Amelie had left their corridor.

Amelie wiped fresh tears from her eyes. “At least we have an ensuite now.” The two of them didn’t seem surprised when Aaron explained how the rooms had moved overnight.

The three of them sat cuddled on a sofa as the morning passed, they even joined in cheering as doors began to appear on the first year wall. The Earth, Air, Water and Fire doors first. Then the Healer door, followed by the Earth Water dual mage door and lastly the Water Fire dual door.

"Wow, a Water Fire dual mage. That's rare." One of the new fourth year dual mages said.

"At least Professor Stein will be happy." Aaron muttered to Tala and Amelie.

Then the room went deathly silent, and every eye turned to Aaron.

The All-Power door had just opened up.

Printed in Great Britain
by Amazon